Just Plain Bob

Hot Erotica
∽
Short Stories,
Vol. 12

Doing What
She Does
Best

WARNING

This book contains sexually explicit scenes and adult language. It may be considered offensive to some readers. This book is for sale to adults ONLY.

Please store your files wisely where they cannot be accessed by underage readers.

* * * * * * * * * * * * * * * * * * *

About the Publisher

4Fun Publishing, a member of **BLVNP Incorporated**, 340 S. Lemon #6200, Walnut CA 91789, info@blvnp.com / legal@blvnp.com
NOTE: Due to the highly emotional reaction of some people to works of erotic fiction, any email sent to the above address that contains foul language or religious references is automatically deleted by our anti-spam software and will not be seen. All other communications are welcome.

DISCLAIMER

Please don't be stupid and kill yourself. This book is a work of FICTION. Do not try any new sexual practice that you find in this book. It is fiction and not to be confused with reality. Neither the author nor the publisher or its associates assume any responsibility for any loss, injury, death or legal consequences resulting from acting on the contents in this book. Every character in this book is over 18 years of age. The author's opinions are not to be construed as the opinions of the publisher. The material in this book is for entertainment purposes ONLY. Enjoy.

Erotica Short Stories, Vol. 12
Doing What She Does Best
Hot Erotica

By: Just Plain Bob

© **Just Plain Bob 2015**
ISBN: 978-1-68030-337-7

Dear Abby

Another Letter To Dear Abby

Mae Goes To Work

A Trip To Clintonville

Nancy's X-Mas Party

Rae Goes For The Money

Dear Abby

Dear Abby,

When I was younger, a lot younger (just turned eighteen actually), I was really stupid. I used drugs and eventually became a prostitute to feed my drug habit. During that period of my life I had so little self-esteem that I allowed men (and women) to do what they wanted with me as long as they gave me the money I needed for my next fix. I got pregnant twice and had two abortions, the last of which ended in my getting a hysterectomy.

It started out as a lot of fun. Several boys that I dated were into pot, they talked me into trying some and I did. It made me mellow and I saw things in a nice rosy glow, but it also put me in a very susceptible condition and when one of the guys made a move on me I just laid back and said "groovy." Before long every guy at school was showing me his stash of 'killer weed' and asking me out for a date; a date that consisted of the guy getting me high and then collecting his reward for keeping me high.

This went on for several months before one night my date took me to a college fraternity party. I got high that night too and when I woke up the next morning I was naked and laying on a dirty mattress on a floor. I found out later that I had been used by seventeen guys that night and some of them had used me more than once. I started to get up and I heard someone say, "Hey, she's awake" and several naked guys came into the room. They were passing a bong around and they gave it to me and I took a hit and then another, and another and pretty soon the guys were between my legs. Sometime later that night somebody put me in a cab and sent me home. Luckily for me my parents were out of town for the weekend and I didn't have to worry about them making a stink. When I woke up the next morning my pussy was sore and I hurt when I walked and I swore that I wasn't ever going to let that happen to me again.

But the next Friday I went out on a date and the same thing happened. This time my parents were home and I caught holy hell for staying out all night. It's a good thing that they didn't know what I'd done or they would have locked me in the basement for six months. As it was I wasn't allowed to date again for two months. The guys must have missed my easy pussy and didn't want to get cut off again because when I started dating again they always made sure I got home on time.

My parents went out of town a lot, leaving me and my older sister home alone. My sister and I had an agreement - we each went our own separate way and we kept our mouths shut. On the weekends my parents were gone, so was I. I was high from the time my date picked me up and I barely knew what happened from then until I woke up the next day. I did know that my pussy got used - got used a lot! Before I knew it, I was the gangbang girl for three different fraternities and I didn't care as long as they gave me what I needed to stay high.

Then the AIDS and herpes scare came along and all of a sudden I didn't seem to be popular anymore. Without guys giving me pot, my life got back to that of a fairly normal eighteen-year-old and I finished high school, met a nice guy and got married. For a year everything was cool and then my husband got transferred to the afternoon shift. One night one of his friends, who didn't know about the shift change, stopped by. I hadn't been adapting well to being alone in the evening and so I asked his friend to stay and have a cup of coffee with me. I didn't mean for anything to happen - I just wanted some company - but his friend took out a baggie and asked me if I would mind his lighting up.

"Not as long as you share," I said. Before he left that night I had sucked his cock twice and he had fucked me three times including once in the ass.

After that he started coming over every night that Tom worked. I would get high and Al would have sex with me. After a week Al showed up with a buddy and by the end of the third week I was getting high and pulling trains for Al. That went on for about six months and then one night Tom came home and found me with a cock in my ass, in my pussy and in my mouth. There were also five other guys waiting for their turn and when Tom tried to break things up, they tied him to a chair in the dining room. I was so high that I didn't know that it had happened until I woke up in the morning and found Tom. He tossed me out onto the street and Al took me in and for the next two months I stayed high and fucked whoever Al brought me.

It was the night of my twenty-first birthday that things got really bad for me. Al threw a party for me that ended up with my getting high and with guys depositing gifts in me. I vaguely remembered the first six guys and then it got very hazy. I remember hearing portions of conversations, but I had no idea what they meant at the time: "…is young, ain't she." "How much you…" "Anyone going to miss…" and then I woke up and found myself on a cot in a windowless room. When I tried the door I found that it was locked so I beat on the door and hollered for someone to let me out. Finally I heard a key in the lock and the door swung open and three black men came in. They didn't say anything, two of them just took my arms and held me while the third did something with a hypodermic needle and then came toward me. I started kicking and screaming and the two guys holding me pushed me back on the cot and held me down while the third man stuck the needle in my arm.

I never left that room or saw clothes for the next week or so. There were injections every day, followed by euphoria and a steady stream of men who did whatever they wanted with me. Black, white, Asian, Mexican, they all took my ass, my mouth or my pussy. Then one day no one came into the room, not to use me or to give me an injection. It wasn't long before my skin began to itch and then it almost seemed like my skin began to crawl and I began crying, beating on the door and begging someone to come and help me. After a couple of hours of absolute misery, the door opened and one of the black guys came in. He prepared my dose, gave it to me and I immediately felt better. The man said:

"You need this," and he held up the needle, "and that means you need me. And here is what you are going to do if you want me to help when you start feeling bad."

What I had to do was give my body to whoever he said. His name was Washington; he was my pimp and I was his whore.

That's the way it was for the next two years. I did whatever I was told to do and I was rewarded with what I had to have. I did not go quietly into the life; twice I broke away, but it did me no good. The first time I managed to get home, but my parents threw me out, called me a worthless druggie and a whore and slammed the door in my face. By noon the next day I was begging Washington to help me because I was sure that I was going to die. Five months later I tried again and was hooking on my own to earn money for a fix, but I couldn't find anyone that would sell to me and I ended up crawling back to Washington.

After that I gave up any thought of trying to get away and settled in to be the punch board for everyone willing to pay Washington for the privilege; twosomes, threesomes and foursomes were common place and gangbangs were the norm rather than the exception. I was made to sit in a bathtub and be peed on and I had to straddle the tub and do the peeing and there were lots of other things that I had to do that were too disgusting to write about.

Then one day a miracle occurred; I was being gangbanged during a high stakes poker game and the police raided the place. A couple of people at the game told the cops that I was being paid to be there and I was arrested and given six months. The good part was that I was given treatment for my drug problem. I have been clean for almost a full year now and I've met the most wonderful man and we have a great relationship. He wants to marry me and my question is: Should I tell him about my past or cross my fingers and hope to God he never finds out?

End of the 1st Story

Another Letter to Dear Abby

Dear Abby,

I am a 44-year-old woman and I will have been married to my husband for 25 years this coming Thursday. I love my husband dearly, but I have kept a secret (actually two of them) from him for our entire marriage.

My husband and I dated for about three years and we were due to be married. Although we did make love, it wasn't a regular thing. I had waited until he proposed before I gave up my virginity, but he worked out of town a lot and we both still lived with our parents so there wasn't a lot of opportunity. I think that all total that we had made love maybe eight times over a five-month period.

The week before the wedding, the girls I work with threw a small party for me at a local lounge. They bought me drinks and made me dance with whatever guy who came to our table. It didn't matter if the guy came to ask Debbie, Carol, Alice or Bev; he got me. I'd had enough drinks to get "loose" and when the guys felt me up I didn't fight their hands off. I didn't care because I knew that none of them were going to get lucky. Not with all of the girls I worked with being right there and watching.

After almost two hours at the lounge, Alice said that it was time to give me my surprise and when I asked where it was, they said we had to go get it.

We got up and left the lounge and got in Carol's Suburban and as she started the car Alice said, "Here, honey. As part of the surprise you have to wear this," and she produced a blindfold.

I was blindfolded and about five minutes later we parked and I was led inside a building where loud music was playing. I was led to a seat and the blindfold was removed and I saw that we were in a strip club and it was male dancers night.

I looked around the club and saw that almost all the patrons were women although a few of them did appear to have men with them. I was frankly amazed at the way a good part of those women behaved as the men took off their costumes as they danced. Some of them had to be restrained when they tried to get up on the stage with the dancers.

There were cries of "Take it all off and show us what you got" and "Show us the package baby." The girls fed me drinks and made lewd comments like:

"Look at the lump in his thong. Is your guy hung like that?"

Alice pointed at one of the dancers and said:

"Doesn't he look yummy? Wouldn't you just love to eat him up?"

He did look pretty good and for a second or so I let my imagination run wild. I'd had about five drinks since we got there and those on top of what I'd had before we got there so I was feeling no pain. I was getting into the spirit of things and was chanting "Show us the beef stick, show us the beef stick" with the other women when Carol said:

"Here he comes."

"Here who comes?"

"Your surprise, honey. The reason we brought you here."

She pointed and I saw one of the dancers walk up. He looked like a Greek god and my tummy got all fluttery.

"This is Toby, honey, and Toby is going to give you a lap dance. I know he is yummy and I can tell from the look in your eyes that you want to do something naughty, but the rules are that you can look, but you can't touch."

Toby proceeded to give me a lap dance and when he was finished I was weak in the knees when he got up and if he had wanted to take me right there on the table in front of God and everybody, I would have let him. After Toby walked away, I told the girls I needed to use the ladies room and I got up to go. Alice got up to go with me and after taking care of our business and while we were touching up our makeup, Alice asked me if after seeing all those sexy male dancers I really wanted to get married and settle for just one guy. I laughed and told her that maybe I could talk hubby into letting me keep a spare in the garage.

"Got one in mind?"

"I think Toby would do nicely."

When Alice and I walked out of the bathroom, we found Toby leaning against the wall waiting for us. He said that the girls at the table had told him that I was getting married next week and I told him that I was. He said he had a special lap dance for women who were about to get married and then he said to follow him to one of the private rooms and he would give it to me. Alice raised her eyebrows at that and Toby told her that he would see to it that I got back to the table.

He took my hand and led me to a small room that held a table, a straight backed chair and a small stand in one corner with a cassette player on it. Pushed up against one wall was a sturdy looking table. He closed the door behind us and locked it and told me to sit down on the chair. He hit the play button on the cassette recorder and music filled the room. He started on the lap dance and it had the same effect on me in that little room that it had had on me out in the lounge.

My panties got wet!

As he performed, Toby whispered to me that the rules that pertained to lap dances in the lounge didn't hold in the little room. He pointed out that there was no window and that the door was locked so that whatever took place in the room would be between the people in the room and no one else. He stepped out of his thong and kicked it into one of the corners and then said I could even touch if I wanted.

As he swayed and moved and rubbed himself against me in time to the music, I stared at his cock as it bobbed around and felt the same way I had felt out in the lounge.

If he wanted to take me, I would let him.

I reached out and my fingers touched his hard maleness and Toby smiled and said that he knew it; he had smelled it on me out in the lounge. He pulled me off the chair and bent me forward over the table and then worked my panties down and I stepped out of them. I was hot, horny and feeling no pain from all the drinks that I'd had. He pushed my skirt up to my waist and his knees spread my legs apart and then he slid his manhood into my vagina. As he worked himself into me, his fingers unbuttoned my blouse and he pushed my bra down so that my breasts were hanging free and then he began rolling my nipples between his thumbs and forefingers.

I was gasping for breath and moaning as he drove himself into me. He pounded into me and I cried out as he gave me orgasm after orgasm. Then he told me that he was ready to give me my wedding present and I felt his juices boil out of him and into me. He slid his softening cock out of me and I felt abandoned and empty and I wished he could have lasted longer. Before I could lift myself from the table, he moved back between my legs and pushed his hard cock back into me. Then a voice that wasn't Toby's told me that he was surprised that I was still so tight even after I'd had a load pushed into me.

I rose up enough to look back over my shoulder and I saw that it was another one of the dancers who was doing me. I saw Toby heading for the door and he smiled at me and said:

"I know I said the door was locked, but I never said I was the only one with a key," and he opened the door and left the room. It was then that I saw two more dancers standing there watching and I suddenly realized that I was going to be gangbanged. I was surprised that the thought didn't make me fight to get up from that table.

The man doing me gave me another climax before he gave me his 'wedding present' and then he backed away and another dancer moved in and took his place. He too gave me an orgasm and a 'wedding present' before pulling away. The next dancer got me up on the table and on my back. He lifted my legs up on his shoulders and then slammed his cock into me. Another dancer moved up by my head and pushed his cock in my mouth and started fucking my face and I heard the dancer fucking me tell the others in the room that I was loving it and I guess I was because I was pushing back at him as he drove down into me.

I have no idea how many men had me in that little room or how many of them went once, twice or more times, but eventually I was alone in the room, flat on my back on the table and wondering what train had just hit me.

But my night wasn't yet over.

Toby came back and told me that he had told my friends that he would see to it that I got home and then he took me to his apartment where he and three of his friends did me until six the next morning. When Toby dropped me off at home, I could barely walk and for the next two days I didn't. I soaked in the tub and rested up. The unplanned outcome of that night was that I was pregnant when I returned from the honeymoon and I know that the father of my child was one of the dancers. That secret I'll take to my grave.

That night woke something up in me and turned me into slut. I saw Toby three more times before the wedding - the last time the night before I walked down the aisle - and he continued to see me on the average of twice a week for the next three years until he moved out of state.

I do confess that Toby wasn't the last of my lovers, just one of many. There have been many others over the years, usually men I work with and strangers I meet in hotels and bars when I'm out of town on business trips or my hubby is gone on trips and all without my husband knowing anything about it.

My problem, Abby, is that as I get older my sexual urges are increasing. I'm doing a gangbang on the average of every two weeks and I'm doing co-workers in the supply closet at work almost daily. It is inevitable that if I keep it up, I'm going to get caught by my husband.

My question is, "Do you think my husband would understand my need to be a slut if I confessed to him?"

The End

Mae Goes to Work

My company wanted to send me to Denver to take care of a problem at our Denver office. I did not really want to make the trip because I had already spent five of the previous six weeks on the road. I told my boss that I really needed to stay home for a while because of personal problems. He told me three days couldn't possibly make a difference and when I told him that even three hours could make a difference, he asked for an explanation.

My wife, Mae, had recently celebrated a birthday and was now, as she put it, on the uncomfortable side of forty-five. This might not seem like a major complaint to some, but a few other things, combined with passing forty-five, had put Mae down in the dumps. Mae has been a sexy woman all her life and her life has been filled with males coming on to her. Recently, however, she says the wolf whistles have stopped, men no longer pay her any attention and she has come to believe she is old and undesirable. Basically, her self-esteem was going into the toilet.

During my last two business trips a couple of events occurred that convinced her that what she was feeling about herself was true. With our own kids grown up and gone and me away on business, Mae's main social outlet is her girl friends. She had gone out with them one night, following a bridal shower, and they had stopped at a local lounge for drinks. The lounge had a live band and while all of Mae's friends had been asked to dance at least once, no one had paid any attention to Mae. She had brooded about it for a week and when the same thing happened the following week, she just knew she was right - she was old and no longer desirable. It bothered her so much, in fact, that one night she had gone out and tried to get herself picked up, but had no takers.

After my last trip, I had noticed how cranky and irritable she had become and after bugging her about it, she had unloaded her feelings. So, I needed to stay home and spend some time with her - I had to convince her that her life wasn't over. I didn't want to sound like I was overly alarmed, but given the way she was behaving I couldn't rule out suicide if she was left home alone.

My boss looked thoughtful for a moment before saying, "I don't want this to sound crude, Robert, but you do know, don't you, that there isn't a man in this office who knows Mae who wouldn't take a shot at her if he thought he could get away with it?"

I nodded that, yes, I was aware. I knew how desirable Mae was; after twenty-six years of marriage, Mae could still make my blood boil with nothing more than a sidelong glance.

"Tell you what I can do," Dave said. "We can use some part-time help here at the office. See if Mae would be interested - it would get her out of the house, give her something to do, and the boys in the office will give her all the wolf whistles she can handle."

Mae was a bit reluctant at first since she had been out of the work force for quite a while, but she eventually decided to give it a try. I was in town for her first week on the job and I could see an immediate improvement in her attitude. When I left for a three-day trip to Salt Lake City, I left feeling that I had nothing more to worry about. I returned from Salt Lake around seven Friday evening and when I got home Mae wasn't there. She got home around ten and I could tell she had been drinking. She told me she had stopped after work for a few drinks with the people from the office and then they had gone to dinner.

"Have a good time?" I asked.

"Oh yes. Taking this job has really been good for me. I'm glad you are home, Sweetie, cause I'm horny as hell. Race you to bed!"

Boy was she wet when I entered her; she would have fucked all night if I could have stayed with her.

Mae was her old self again, but there was a major change in her - she was horny all the time. When I'd get home she would drag me off to the bedroom before I even had a chance to put my suitcase down. She would wake me up in the morning with blowjobs and on one trip I took, she drove me to the airport and had me fuck her in the back seat of the car in the parking lot.

About a month after Mae started working for the company, I received a promotion to Regional Manager. It came as a complete surprise to me because, even though I had wanted the job, I did not think I was even on the list of those being considered. The new job meant more money, but it also meant more time on the road. At first I was afraid that the promotion was going to cause a problem between Mae and me, but she was now working full-time and she said we would find a way to work things out. Life was good - I was making good money, Mae was happy, and our sex life was fantastic. The only real problem, at least from my standpoint, was that I was spending more time on the road at a time when Mae's sexual appetite seemed to be increasing.

Yesterday, Mae drove me to the airport for a 12:30 flight. I kissed her goodbye and told her to keep her 'honey pot' warm for me. She laughed and said, "Warm hell! I'll keep it red hot!" As I sat in the waiting area waiting for my flight to be called, I wondered if I should give up the job and spend more time at home with Mae. We didn't need the extra money and all the sex we were having had me feeling like a kid again. My thoughts were interrupted by an announcement that my flight was going to be delayed for at least forty-five minutes because of a maintenance problem. An hour later they announced an additional delay of an hour and thirty minutes; after that they announced that my flight was cancelled. They tried to reroute me on another airline, but I would have had to fly to Chicago, change planes for a flight to Denver, and then change planes again for the flight to Seattle. I decided to wait and go the next day. I caught the shuttle bus back into the city and took a cab to my office. The office was closed for the day, but as long as I was still in town I thought I would get the latest sales figures and review them before going home. I let myself in and as I was going toward my office, I heard noises coming from Norm's office. As I got closer, the noises turned into voices and I heard "Harder, harder, fuck me harder. Oh God - yes - I love your cock!"

"Oho," I thought. "Norm's getting a little on the side. He better hope Naomi (his wife) never comes in on him like this."

Curious to see who who he was nailing, I crept forward and peeked around the doorjamb - and froze. I was absolutely stunned to see Norm pounding his stiff dick into Mae and from the sounds Mae was making, she was loving it. I watched for a good five minutes as Norm fucked my wife and as Mae begged for him to never stop. When finally he did finish and get up from her, I was amazed to see Mae dip a finger in her cunt, bring it out covered in sperm, and then take it to her mouth and lick it. Norm put his pants back on and told Mae he would swing by our house later that evening, but Mae told him he couldn't.

"Why not? Robert is out of town, right?"

"Yes, but you forgot that you asked me to go out with Pettigrew tonight. He's picking me up at seven and by the time he gets through with me, you'll have to be home in bed with Naomi."

"Damn! You're right. I'd forgotten about that. Well, you be sure to take good care of him - he's one of our best customers. While we are on the subject, can you leave Wednesday open for Gil Howe?"

"I don't know. Robert might be home Wednesday night."

Norm said, "I'll make a phone call and see that he doesn't get home till Thursday."

I was shocked at what I was hearing. My wife was not only fucking my boss, but she was servicing our customers too? I slowly moved away and caught a cab home. I was going to be there when Mae got home.

I was sitting in the den with the lights out when I heard Mae come in. I heard her run up the stairs and a minute later the shower started running. I looked at my watch and saw that Pettigrew was due in thirty minutes. I'd had a lot to think about while waiting for her to get home - about us, about the job, but mostly about us and I didn't much like my thoughts. I was very happy with Mae's increased sexual appetite and it was obvious that whatever she was doing on the side was a major part of it.

Our personal relationship was not suffering because of her extracurricular activities - on the contrary, we were fucking more now than ever before. Mae always seemed to be very happy to see me when I came home and sorry to see me leave. I guess what I was really asking myself was, could I live with what I had just found out? What would happen if I put my foot down and stopped it? The shower stopped and I still sat pondering on what to do. On the one hand, I was pissed that Mae was fucking around on me. On the other, I could not put out of my mind the way I had felt watching her fuck Norm. The truth was that it had excited me! I looked at my watch again - five minutes till Pettigrew.

I walked upstairs and into the bedroom. Mae was standing in front of the mirror, clad only in nylons, garterbelt, high heels, black lace panties and bra and applying make-up.

"My, don't we look sexy," I said. Mae was startled and turned to look at me with confusion on her face. "My flight was cancelled," I told her.

Just then the doorbell rang and I looked at my watch. "There's Pettigrew - right on time."

Mae's face turned ashen. She started to speak, but I held up my hand." I don't know what your plans were. Out to dinner? Dancing? Go to his hotel room or bring him back here? Doesn't matter. This is how it is going to go. You put on your negligee, go downstairs and bring him up here. Then you do whatever he wants while I watch from the closet. After that you go on out on your date. While you're gone, I'm going to sit in the den and think about things – us, in particular. If he wants more of your pussy give it to him, but make sure that you are home by six a.m. We are going to have a long talk before I leave to catch my flight - if I leave to catch a flight."

Mae just stood and looked at me. The doorbell rang again. "Go"

I said, "We mustn't keep Pettigrew waiting."

She took one last look at me and went downstairs to get Pettigrew and I got in the closet and adjusted things so I could get a good view. Mae was back in minutes with a rather nice looking gentleman of about forty (I would have to remember to rib Mae about robbing the cradle) and she cast several nervous glances my way until Pettigrew took over. He slipped her negligee off and stood back to admire the view. Mae did a slow turn in front of him and stepped forward to begin helping him remove his clothes. Once naked, he pushed her back onto the bed and when she sat down, he removed her black lace panties, spread her legs and leaned down to begin licking her pussy. Mae loves having her cunt eaten and Pettigrew must have known what he was doing because Mae was moaning in less than a minute and had her first orgasm in less than two. Then the two of them settled down for some serious fucking. Mae had two more orgasms while I watched and I could not believe how erotic she looked with her legs up over her shoulders, high heels pointing at the ceiling, while Pettigrew fuck her with hard, fast strokes.

Pettigrew took a good ten minutes before he came - I beat him by two, but it was going to cost me a large dry cleaning bill because I shot all over half the stuff in the closet. I had never been so turned on in my life. The two of them dressed, Mae freshened up her lipstick and they left on their date. I watched them from the bedroom window as they climbed into a limo and headed up the street. I sat in my den for hours trying to sort out my thoughts - my emotions were mixed to say the least. I was mad, I was jealous, I was turned on. I had never felt as much lust for my wife as I had felt watching her take Pettigrew into her hot cunt.

The sound of a car door slamming woke me up and I looked at the clock - 5:45. The front door opened, closed, and I heard Mae going up the stairs. I got up and followed her; she hesitantly entered the bedroom and when she didn't see me, she turned around and gave a start when she saw me behind her.

"Take off your dress." She looked at me at me with frightened eyes. "Do it!" I said. She dropped her clutch purse on the floor and pulled her dress off. She was not wearing panties and her bush was matted with cum. "No panties?"

"He kept them," came out as a whisper.

I pushed her back onto the bed. My cock was already out and as I moved between her legs, I said, "Put it in." She looked at me confused. "Put it in. Put my cock into your unfaithful hole."

She reached down and guided me into her wet and sloppy cunt and I started to fuck her with slow hard strokes, but the sensation my cock felt in that sperm filled pit soon had me fucking her like a mad man. She was moaning now, not words, but a series of low sounds - almost like low grunts. I fucked harder - I was trying to drive myself straight through her. Her moans became cries of "Fuck me. Fuck me. Fuck me. Harder. Oh God harder, harder, please fuck me harder."

And I did, Lord did I ever, but I could not cum. I was hard as a rock and I craved release, but I could not get off. Mae was hollering, "Oh god oh god oh god fuck me oh god fuck me," and her nails were dug in my back, her legs were locked around my hips and she was pushing up at me as hard as I was driving down into her. She had at least two orgasms that I was aware of and probably more that I missed, but I was concentrating solely on my own relief. I could not get the picture of Pettigrew's cock moving in and out of her while her legs kicked in the air out of my mind. It was the image of his final thrust that sent me over the edge. I came so hard that it hurt. For a few moments I held myself steady over Mae as I tried to catch my breath and then I rolled off her.

There were several moments of silence before Mae spoke, "Jesus, Robert. What got into you?"

"What got into me is what's been getting into you!"

More silence. "Robert, I…"

"No!" I said. "First you tell me about your night. I want to hear it all - step by step." Still more silence. I looked over at her. "Tell me. I want to know."

Hesitantly she started to talk. They had gotten into the limo and before they were two blocks away from the house, he had her sucking his cock. He had let the partition down so the limo driver could watch in the mirror and he had cum in her mouth just as they reached the restaurant where they were to have dinner. Following a leisurely dinner they had driven to a local nightclub where they had spent several hours drinking and dancing. Then they went to his hotel where he had fucked her twice more. She left the hotel at four-thirty to come home, but halfway home the limo had pulled over and the chauffeur had gotten in back with her. Mae had been somewhat fearful because the chauffeur was a black man and Mae was from a racist family in Alabama, but she had reluctantly sucked his cock and then enthusiastically let him fuck her. She fell quiet as I lay there looking at the ceiling.

"How long have you known?" Mae asked me.

"Since yesterday when I came back to the office and saw you with Norm. How long has it been going on?"

Mae gave a little half smile as she thought back. "Since the first trip you took after I started working."

Why?" I asked. "I mean, how did it start?"

Mae told me how the people at the office had asked her to join them after work for a drink. She had stopped with them and for a few hours they drank, talked and danced, and pretty soon Mae was the only female left and she was getting all the attention. She'd had a few too many drinks and Toby, one of her co-workers, had suggested they go outside for some fresh air. They had sat in his car and talked for a bit and suddenly they were kissing and the next thing she knew she was giving him a blowjob. Later, back inside the bar, she had a few more drinks and while she was dancing with Ben, he asked her if she would go out back with him. At first she had said no, but after a few more drinks and a lot of pleading from Ben, she had said ok and they had gone out to his car. She was sucking his cock when she looked up and saw that the other three guys from work were standing there and watching. She finished sucking off Ben and when he got up, another guy made as if to take his place. Mae had said no. She didn't want to get caught giving blowjobs in the parking lot so the guys had driven her home. She told them blowjobs only and they had agreed, but one thing had led to another and they ended up taking turns fucking her.

The next day at work it had been business as usual and the guys had treated her as they would have any other co-worker and when they asked her to stop after work for a drink, she had declined. At home she had just stepped out of the shower when the doorbell rang. She had answered the door to find Ben, Toby, and Fred standing on the porch with two pizzas and a case of beer. They said they had come to apologize for taking advantage of her when she was too high to know what she was doing, and to ask for forgiveness. She let them in and before an hour was up they were taking turns with her again.

The following Monday Norm had asked her to come into his office at the end of the day. He said he had heard that she had developed a good rapport with her fellow workers and she had nodded yes. He then said he didn't want to be left out and they ended up fucking on his desk. The next day he had a couch put in his office and he had fucked her on it every day since and every day since she would stop for drinks after work and usually go home with someone or take someone home with her. Then Norm had asked her for a favor - there was an important client in town for a few days and he was at loose ends - would Mae have dinner with him? She had, and they had ended up in his hotel room - for two days. Norm had asked her for the same favor several more times and always with the same result. Just yesterday Norm had given her a check for $7500; he told her she had been responsible for his landing several lucrative contracts and she should consider the check as either a bonus or a commission.

I stared at the ceiling as I considered what she'd told me. I was surprised that I was not furious with her, that I did not feel any jealousy toward my co-workers or Norm. The strongest feeling I had was anger at the job that was keeping me away while all this was going on. But then again, if I had stayed home it never would have happened.

"What now?" asked Mae.

"What now indeed?" I thought as I sat up in bed. "I have a plane to catch and you have a job to go to. I'll expect you to call me at my hotel and fill me in on the details of your date with Howe," and I headed for the shower.

The End

A Trip to Clintonville

This is a wimp story in that the wife cheated, the husband found out and did nothing about it. If you don't like this kind of story just move on to the next one and save yourself from turning purple with rage and wasting your valuable time writing silly comments that will be ignored anyway. That won't stop Harry, but who pays any attention to him anyway.

***

Nancy and I have been married a little over nine years and they have been damned good years. Nan is a great mother to our three children, and excellent housekeeper and cook and she spoils me rotten. Our sex life has slowed down some since we were married. The hot monkey jungle sex that we enjoyed for our first four years has tapered off to three times a week, but occasionally on some of those times we do manage to get it on two or even three times. I have no complaints – not a one.

When I asked Nancy to marry me she was reluctant to say yes, but I kept pressing her and finally she said that she didn't want to saddle me with a girl who had a history of being a slut. When she told me that, I wasn't too surprised since she had given it up to me on our first date, but in all honesty that is why I had asked her out in the first place. The word was she was an easy piece and I hadn't been laid in a while so I asked her out.

I was surprised when I felt a spark when we kissed and before the night was over the little whore pretty much had me wanting her for my own. There are those who will smirk and say I was young and stupid and that all it was my dick saying:

"Hey bud, got some easy pussy here so let's keep her around for as long as we can."

It wasn't that way. I felt that we had really connected and I was sure that she felt that way too since she didn't date anyone but me after that night. Anyway, when I told her I didn't give a rat's ass about anything she had done before me, she insisted that I know the full story before she would give me an answer to my proposal. I know she expected me to run screaming from her when she unburdened herself, but I knew that it wouldn't happen.

Her story started on her eighteenth birthday. Her parents threw a party for her and one of the guys who came to the party managed to get her alone and he had taken her cherry. She had liked it so much that she had snuck away with him an hour later and they had done it again. After the party broke up, he took her out for a ride and she told him to find a place to park because she wanted to do it again. He told her okay, but that he would need help in getting it back up and she asked what she could do. He told her and Nancy gave her first blow job. She liked it and after that there was no holding back and she developed a reputation as a "fantastic cocksucker" among the guys she dated.

The guy who had taken her cherry was home on leave and they screwed like sex crazed rabbits until his leave was up and two days after he had returned to duty a guy asked her out and she gave it up to him before the end of the date. He fucked her every time they could get together until they graduated in May and he went off to the Navy. Before going he told a buddy how great she was at giving head and how easy it was to get her panties off so the buddy moved in, screwed her through the summer until Nancy went off to college in the fall.

Over the next three years she went through so many guys she couldn't even remember them all. Along the way she tried some threesomes, foursomes and several gangbangs. She loved to fuck and she loved to suck cock. Three nights before she went out with me for the first time she did a gangbang with nine guys. When she finished telling me that, I smiled and said:

"I guess you have done a few more than I have, but that probably means you learned a lot more so you will have to spend the early part of our marriage teaching me what I don't know."

"Are you serious? You still want me knowing all that?"

"Is it over?"

"Oh God yes. You are all that I need."

"That's good enough for me. Pick a date."

Nine years later and I was pretty damned sure that Nancy had never broken her wedding vows. No, that isn't right; I was certain that she hadn't.

***

Her parents lived three hours away and every six weeks or so we would drive over to visit and let them spend some time with their grandkids. We never spent time visiting with others so after nine years of marriage I knew very few of her friends that she had grown up and gone to school with.

A month ago Nan got a phone call from her mom. Her mom had decided to organize a family reunion and she gave Nan the date that she had chosen. It was on a Saturday and we decided to drive over on Friday night after I got off from work and stay until Sunday afternoon. We pulled into Clintonville around nine and Nan had me stop at a liquor store to pick up a case of beer and a couple bottles of wine. While I was looking through the wine selections I heard an:

"Oh my God! Is that you, Nance?"

I looked over and saw a fairly good looking redhead run up and hug Nan. They started talking and Nan introduced me to Sarah who was one of the girls she had grown up with. The outcome of the little meeting was that we were invited to a party at Sarah's on Saturday night. When I reminded Nancy that we were committed to a family reunion on Saturday, she said there was no problem because the reunion was an all day affair and would probably break up around six and we could hit

Sarah's party at seven.

I met a lot of Nancy's relatives on Saturday and a pretty good time was had by all. Nan was right and the party did start to break up around five-thirty and her folks agreed to babysit so Nan and I could visit with her old friends.

The party was in full swing when we got there and it looked like some of the people there were already in the bag. Sarah introduced us to her husband Tim who apparently had not gone to school with Nan and Sarah. Almost immediately there was a swarm of girls around Nan telling her how great she looked and asking her how she had been. I was introduced to all of them and from the looks I got from some of them I got the impression that they thought she had done okay for herself.

I sort of felt like I was intruding on their little reunion so I wandered away and found a group watching a ball game. Tim was one of them and he introduced me as Nancy's husband and I thought I detected a curious look from a couple of them. I figured they knew her past and wondered if I did. I got into watching the game and drinking beer and talking baseball with the guys.

Maybe an hour later I felt the crying need to use the bathroom and after getting directions I headed for it. I took my whiz and when I came out into the hallway I hesitated just long enough to make sure I'd zipped up my fly and it was then I heard:

"You guys are just so bad."

It was Nan's voice and it came from the room just across the hall from the bathroom. I went to the door and, very quietly and carefully, tried the door knob, but it was locked. While doing that I heard Nan say:

"You know we shouldn't be doing this. My husband wouldn't like this one little bit."

A male voice said, "I'm damned sure not going to tell him. How about you, Hank?"

"I don't even know who he is," said another male voice.

"See?" said the first voice. "He'll never know unless you tell him."

"I can't believe I'm doing this," Nan said.

I had a choice. I could beat on the door until someone opened it. What then? What I'd heard indicated that something I wouldn't like was going on in there, but if they opened the door and were fully clothed they could come up with some lame assed, but slightly plausible explanation and what could I do besides letting them know just how pissed I was. The other choice was to try and find out what was going on in the room.

I studied the layout of the house to orient myself and then went outside. I checked things out and decided where the window to the room would be and I circled around the house to one I thought it would be. Luckily all the partying was going on inside the house so there was no one else around to see what I was doing.

The window was too high for me to see into so I looked around for something to stand on and just short of the front of the house I saw a wheelbarrow with a shovel leaning on it. It looked like Sarah and Tim were putting in a flower bed. I pushed the wheelbarrow over and set it down under the window and stood on it. The blinds were down but there were a couple of gaps that I could see through and I looked into the room.

I saw a fully clothed Nan sitting on the edge of a bed. It being summer even though the blinds were down, the screened window was open so I could hear what was going on as well as see it. Two men were standing in front of Nan and booth were unzipped and had hard cocks sticking out of their flies. Nan was leaning forward and sucking one of the cocks and after a minute she switched to the other guy and sucked his. I stood there with rage building up inside of me. I could have broken it up by yelling through the screen, but why bother. What was done was done. I decided to watch and listen to see if I could learn anything that would help me in the coming divorce.

For the next ten minutes Nan switched back and forth between the two dicks, spending a minute on each one before the switch. Finally the man in her mouth said:

"I'm cumming, Nan; I'm gonna shoot."

Nan grabbed his ass and pulled his cock deep into her mouth and I saw her throat move as she swallowed. Near as I could tell she didn't miss a drop. She kept him in her mouth until he was soft and then she switched to the other guy. As she leaned forward to take him in her mouth, he pushed her head away from his cock and pushed her down on the bed on her back.

"What are you doing" she asked.

He said nothing, but quickly reached under her skirt, grabbed her panties and pulled them off her before she knew what he meant to do. As her panties fell to the floor she understood what he intended and she said:

"No, damn it, no. I said blow jobs only and you agreed."

He laughed and said, "I lied. I'm invoking the cherry popper rule."

"What the hell is that?"

"The rule says that the guy who got your cherry gets to fuck you whenever and wherever he wants."

"But you can't. I'm married and I love my husband."

"Oh yeah? Then what are you doing in here sucking cocks?"

"I just wanted to relive one of my fond memories. I've never screwed another man since I married Frank and I don't intend to start now."

"Tough shit, Nance. The cherry popper rule says I can have your sweet pussy whenever I want it and that would be now."

While he had been talking he had been inching forward so he was between her legs and when she said, "No damn it; I'm not going to do it, John," and tried to close her legs, she couldn't. His hands were on her shoulders pinning her to the bed and he moved forward with his cock getting closer and closer to her pussy.

"I'll scream, John. I'll scream rape at the top of my lungs if you don't stop this right now."

"Go ahead and when everybody including your husband rushes in, they will all want to know what is going on and I'll have to tell them that you were giving out blow jobs and it got a little out of hand. Is your hubby an open minded kind of guy? Will he be happy to know that you were only supposed to be giving blow jobs?"

"Damn it, John; I don't want this."

"But I do, Nance, I most definitely do," and he pushed the head of his cock into her.

She might not have wanted it, but the excitement of giving two of her old lovers blow jobs apparently had gotten her wet because he slid right into her. Nan beat on his shoulders, called him a motherfucker, a bastard and a rotten son of a bitch, but he ignored her and pounded her pussy. Again I could have broken it up by yelling through the window, but I was pissed that she was in the room passing out blow jobs in the first place so if he was doing her against her wishes, that was just too fucking bad. I just watched as I made mental list of the things I would have to do in divorcing her.

Given Nancy's sexual nature I should have expected what happened next, but I didn't. I was standing there watching and thinking "Serves you right, you cheating whore," when her legs came up and clamped him and her hands grabbed his ass and pulled him to her. She started fucking back up at him and he said:

"That's it, Nance, that's it. Fuck me like you used to, baby; give up that sweet pussy."

Nancy was moaning, "Fuck me, you bastard, fuck me."

The guy still had his pants on and I prayed that Nancy's pussy hairs would get caught in his zipper and cause her some pain, but it didn't happen. After five minutes of hard pounding the guy said:

"Here it comes, Nance; here it comes," and he apparently blew his load.

Nancy was crying, "Not yet, not yet damn it, not yet. Get me off, damn it, get me off."

The guy said, "Sorry, Nance; no can do."

While cherry popper had been fucking Nancy, the other guy had taken off his pants and watching had gotten him up again. He stepped up behind CP and tapped him on the shoulder. CP looked back and smiled and quickly stepped away from Nancy as she cried out, "God damn you!" Before the "you" was out of her mouth, the second guy plunged into her. Nancy's eyes shot open in surprise and for maybe a tenth of a second, according to her facial expression anyway, she thought of telling him to get the fuck off of her, but then the legs came up and clamped and the hands grabbed and she cried:

"Make me cum; get me off, fuck me and get me off."

Less than a minute later Nancy had an orgasm. The guy had already cum down her throat so he was lasting a while and soon had

Nancy working up to her second orgasm. She and the guy came together and as the guy started to pull away from her, she grabbed him and tried to hold him in her. Cherry popper said:

"She's on fire. Go get Sam and Bill."

Cherry popper climbed on the bed as the guy pulled out of Nancy, dressed and quickly left the room. CP pushed his cock at Nancy's mouth and said:

"Get me up again, Nance. Us your magic mouth to get me up while Al goes to get some help."

Nancy took CP's cock in her mouth and just as he said, "Damn, Nance, you give the best head ever," she bit down on his cock – hard!! He yelled and pulled away from her and she rolled to the right, stood up and grabbed the table lamp off the bedside stand and slammed it up against cherry popper's head. He hit the floor and Nancy ripped the lamp cord out of the wall to free the lamp and then she smashed it into his crotch three or four times as she screamed at him:

"I said "no", you motherfucker. I told you no. You made me cheat on my husband, you fucking asshole, and you have to pay for that." She smashed him two more times in the family jewels and said, "The next time a girl says no, you had better fucking listen to her."

She tossed the lamp aside, picked up her panties and put them on. She headed for the door, stopped and came back to the moaning man on the floor and kicked him hard one more time in the crotch. "That one is for my husband, you low life shit," and she left the room. I got off the wheelbarrow and hurried back to the guys watching the ball game.

***

I rejoined the group watching the game and it didn't seem like I'd been missed. Maybe five minutes later Nan came up to me with a glass of wine in her hand and asked me if I was getting along okay and I said I was. She apologized for abandoning me:

"But I haven't seen some of these people in ten or twelve years and God only knows when I might get to see them again."

I tried to keep the tone of my voice from sounding sarcastic when I said:

"No problem. Just go ahead and enjoy yourself."

"You're the best, baby," she said as she kissed me. Thank God her mouth tasted like the wine she was drinking. I don't know what I would have done if the kiss would have had the salty taste of sperm. I assumed, or maybe hoped, that when she left the bedroom she went straight across the hall to the bathroom and cleaned up. I would know for sure when we left and got back to her parents' house. I knew she would be horny and want to play, but she wouldn't want me to feel the two loads of cum in her snatch. So, if she put me off I'd know that she hadn't cleaned herself up and if she didn't put me off I would know she was clean. Of course all that overlooked the fact that I just might not want to have anything to do with the cheating slut anyway.

I kept an eye on her for the rest of the party. Cherry popper never made an appearance, but I saw that the other guy was still there. Once I saw Nan heading toward him and he saw her coming and hurried away in the other direction. I guess he had returned to the room and seen what Nan had done to CP and he didn't want a taste of it. She did disappear a couple of times, but never for more than a couple of minutes so I doubted that she'd had enough time to do anything.

I did a lot of thinking while I pretended to watch the ball game. I wasn't all that upset that she had fucked the two guys because I knew that it had started out as non-consensual sex. I couldn't really call it rape because she had started things by sucking their dicks in the first place. The fact that it went from non-consensual on her part to her being an active participant was also something I couldn't hold against her. I knew that with her sexual nature that once CP got her going her body was going to take over and she was going to get into it. I guess I knew how that went. One time before Nan and I got together I'd had sex with a girl and she decided at the last second that she didn't want me to cum in her and she tried to get me to stop, but I was so into it, so close to cumming that there was no way I was going to stop. I just kept pounding to get my nut.

No. What had me the most upset is that she was in that room giving them blow jobs to begin with. A funny thing though. The more I thought about my life with Nan the more I wondered if I really wanted to toss those nine damned good years and a possible thirty or forty more into the trash over two blow jobs she did for old time's sake. Reliving a fond memory, as she had put it. She had admitted to me that she was, and had been, an avid cocksucker before she met me and that she really loved doing it. I guess I could somewhat understand her wanting to relive the experience with the man who had started it all. From the way she treated CP when the fucking was over, there was no doubt in my mind about how she felt about having cheated on me.

Over the course of the evening I saw two guys – one who had been introduced to me as Sam so I guessed the other was Bill – approach Nan and whatever was said didn't seem to set well with them and they walked away from her with sour looks on their faces. Again I was guessing, but I figure that the guy CP sent to fetch them told them what he and CP had done and that Sam and Bill wanted a taste also. From the way they left Nan I'm also guessing that she told them to take a hike.

Once I noticed her off in a corner with Sarah and they were giggling as Nan held her hands about a foot apart. Was she telling Sarah what she had done and was showing Sarah how big the cock of one of the men was? I didn't think that either of them had a dick that big, but then again I hadn't paid all that much attention to the men. I had concentrated on Nan. Sarah laughed and held up a thumb and forefinger about three inches apart and Nan laughed and said something and then she looked around and saw me. She smiled and headed my way. As I watched her walk my way I couldn't get over how sexy she looked and I again wondered if I really wanted to give her up and in an instant the answer came to me.

No, I didn't.

I believe she was telling the truth when she told CP that she loved me and she had never screwed another man since marrying me and didn't intend to. I decided that a couple of blow jobs on old boyfriends to relive a memory weren't worth throwing away nine years of a pretty good marriage. I wasn't brain dead however and I would keep a closer eye on Nan in the future just in case her 'reunion indiscretion' lit a fire she decided that she wanted to feed.

***

"You doing okay?" she asked when she came up to me.

"I'm fine. Having a good time with your old friends?"

"I am. I'm sorry that I haven't kept in closer touch with them. I think that in the future when we come to visit mom and dad we should plan on getting together with some of them."

"Any in particular? Like maybe those old boyfriends you told me about?"

"I can't avoid them, baby. There are seven of them here tonight."

"You sneak off with any of them?" I asked in a joking tone of voice and I saw something quickly flash across her face and then she giggled and said:

"I could have. Several asked me. I still can if you want to see what sloppy seconds from me would be like."

"I don't think so. One of them might make you decide not to come home with me."

"Yeah! As if! You are stuck with me, baby. I remember what I did with all those guys and not one of them could hold a candle to you."

I looked around and asked, "So who are the seven?"

"Oh no you don't. We agreed that what happened before we got together didn't matter. I'm keeping it that way."

"At least tell me which one had the foot long dick."

"I never said that one of them was a foot long."

"Then who were you talking about with Sarah when you were holding your hands about a foot apart?"

"You saw that?"

"I did."

"I was talking about you."

"About me?"

"Sarah knew how big a slut I was and how much I loved to screw and give blow jobs. She wanted to know what was so special about you that I gave up trying to suck and fuck every man in the state. I told her you had a ten-inch cock."

"But I don't have a ten-inch cock."

"Yeah, but she will never know that. At least I don't think she will. She might come after you just to see if I was telling the truth."

"She would do something like that?"

"She might. Back in the day she was as big a slut as I was. She might not have changed."

"She was a slut?"

"Remember me telling you about the gangbang I did just before meeting you?"

I nodded my head yes.

"She was lying on the bed next to me."

I looked over at Sarah and saw that she was looking our way and when she saw me looking at her, she smiled. She was a pretty sexy looking lady. I wondered what I would do if she did come after me. After all, I did have a 'get out of jail free' card thanks to what Nan had done.

"What was the deal with her holding her fingers three inches apart?"

Nan laughed and said, "After I told her how big you were, she told me I was lucky and that she had to settle for three inches."

"She was probably lying too."

"Probably. I do have a confession to make."

I braced myself to hear out herself over her visit to the bedroom with her old boyfriends, but what she said was:

"Seeing my old boyfriends and remembering some of the things we did has me horny as hell. You need to get me out of here and fuck my brains out."

We hadn't even pulled away from the curb when Nan slid over next to me:

"Pay attention to your driving," she said as she worked my cock out of my trousers.

She didn't have enough time to get me off on the short drive to her parents' house and we never made love when we visited because the walls were so thin in the house so she had me pull over on a side street and then she got on the back seat and pulled off her panties as she cried:

"Hurry up, baby, hurry. I need it. I need it bad."

She was soaking wet, but then she always was so I didn't know if she had cleaned herself at Sarah's and I was getting her natural wetness or if I was getting sloppy seconds, but I didn't care. We fucked like a couple of crazed animals in heat.

Oh yeah! No way I was going to get rid of her over a couple of blow jobs, but I would be watching her just in case and you could take that to the bank.

The End

Nancy's X-Mas Party

About an hour from now, Larry, one of my coworkers is going to pay me a visit. I will greet him with a passionate kiss (lots of tongue - he likes that) and then I will take him upstairs to my bedroom. I will do a sexy strip for him (leaving on only my high heels) and then I will help him take off his clothes. I will push him back on the bed, kneel between his legs and give him a slow sensuous blowjob until he comes in my mouth. I will swallow every drop of his sperm, I will lick him clean and I will suck him until he is hard again at which time I will climb into bed with him and spend the next hour or so trying to fuck his brains out. When I have totally satisfied him he will dress and I will walk him down to the front door where he will ask if he can see me again soon. I will smile and tell him that my pussy is his whenever he wants it and I will kiss him goodbye. The door will be barely closed behind him and I will be running up the steps to the bedroom where my husband will be waiting with a rock hard cock, providing, of course, that he didn't jack off in the closet.

How did a thirty-eight-year-old loving wife and mother of three become such a cock-hungry slut? Just pure dumb luck, I guess. It all started last December when my company threw its annual Christmas party. I'd only been with them for three months and I was really looking forward to the party so I could get to know my coworkers better. At the last minute my husband Danny decided to throw cold water on my plans.

"I've been looking forward all year to see these two teams play each other and there is no way I'm going to miss the game for a stupid Christmas party!"

"That's fine," I said, "but I'm going, with or without you!"

The night of the party I didn't bother going home since Danny wasn't going to come; instead I stayed and helped decorate the office. Those of us who were doing the decorating got started sipping the booze right after work and as a consequence we already had a glow on when the rest of the people started arriving. For the rest of the evening, every time I turned around, someone was putting a drink in my hand and I was having a hell of a good time. I danced with several of the men and because of my 'tipsy' condition most of them thought they could get away with grabbing a feel or pushing their hard cocks into my leg or belly, but I pretended to ignore it which only made them bolder. Even when I got caught under the Mistletoe and the kisses got a little heated, I didn't care. After all, I would be going home to Danny and he would be getting all the benefit of the sexual heat that the guys were generating in me. And they were causing me to become hot and bothered; I hadn't had so many hands on my private parts since high school, but I was a big girl now and I knew I could handle these guys.

I'd had quite a bit to drink, but I did not consider that I was drunk, or even close to being drunk so when Larry caught me in the hallway as I was coming back from the ladies room and tried to kiss me, I just giggled and let him. He gave me a little tongue and I gave him a little back. It turned into a passionate embrace and I barely registered that he was walking me backward into the break room. The next thing I knew, Larry had me lying on a table with my dress up around my waist, my panties hanging from an ankle and he was between my legs and working his cock into me. I started to yell but he put his mouth on mine, his tongue was in my throat and then he was fucking me. I struggled, but it wasn't long before my body started to react to what was happening to it. My struggles ceased and my legs came up and locked behind Larry's, my arms went around his neck and then I was pushing back up at him. I don't know how long we were locked together, but eventually I felt him stiffen; I knew he was going to come, but I wasn't ready - I could feel my orgasm coming on - and I begged him to stay with me, but I felt his warmth flood my insides.

"Nooo," I cried as he pulled out and I heard voice say, "Don't worry baby, help is on the way" as a hard cock slid in me. I opened my eyes and saw Don, one of our salesmen, over me and as he began to fuck me hard, I went over the edge. I started down from my high just in time to find Don bringing me right back up. It was the first time in my life that I'd had two orgasms in one session of fucking, but I wasn't finished yet. Don came in me and as soon as he pulled out someone else entered me. I lost count of how many men fucked me that night and how many times I had orgasms. I do know that I was not alone; at one time I looked to my left and saw Alice, our receptionist, being fucked on the table next to me and not by her husband. I found out later that it was her husband who was fucking me while I watched her. Rita, the boss's secretary, was sitting in a chair while Sammy from the mail room ate her pussy and I was vaguely aware of other activity going on in the room. I know Jerry, the forklift driver, came over to my table while someone was fucking me and asked me if he could put his cock in my mouth. I smiled at him and said, "Be my guest" and he was just the first of a half dozen or so who also fucked my face.

All good things come to an end and eventually it was time to go home. In the ladies room I found out from the other girls that all the company parties usually end up the way this one did. Apparently everyone knows what is going to happen and those who don't want to participate leave early and those who stay are assumed to be willing. Not knowing this, I had apparently stayed past the point where the unwilling usually left and everyone had assumed I was fair game.

Even after cleaning up I was a mess when I got home. I had trouble walking from my car to the front porch and as I opened the front door, I prayed Danny would be in bed asleep. No such luck. He was waiting for me in the living room, naked and with a hard on. I looked at him and said:

"Not tonight, Danny. I've had a hard day and I need to get to bed."

"Bullshit! It wasn't a hard day you had - it was hard cocks! The game sucked so I turned it off at the end of the first quarter and drove down to your office to be with you at your party. I got there in time to see the guys lining up on you and I watched you for over an hour as you fucked and sucked them all. Know what? I got turned on watching and it's my turn now!"

And that's how it started. Two or three times a week someone comes over while my husband "is away on business" and we fuck up a storm and when my lover leaves my husband returns from his trip to the closet and we fuck like minks. Oh, and at work? I work directly 'under' the boss now. The fringe benefits are mind blowing.

The End

Rae Goes For The Money

Chapter 1

My sex life pretty much sucked. My wife and I hadn't been getting along all that great recently. Hell, not just recently, but for the last six months! Constant squabbles over money, specifically the lack of it, always seemed to lead in to other areas and we would end up going for days without speaking to each other which translated into no sex. For me it was a no win situation; if I worked a straight forty hours I didn't bring home enough money. If I worked the available overtime or took on a part time job, I caught hell for never being home and for leaving her to raise the kids on her own. One day I'd finally had enough of her bitching and I told her that if she wanted money so god damned bad to get her ass out of the house in the evening and get a job and I'd watch the kids. She started job hunting the next day and the day after that she found one as a tele-marketer - she was going to be the one who interrupted your dinner.

Things got immediately better. I was having a good time being a father to our kids, not that I wasn't one before, but now I did not have to share time with mom, it was just me. Rae was in a much better mood and I think it had as much to do with her being able to get out of the house for a while as it did the money. And with the constant arguments out of the way, I began to have a sex life again.

Rae had a small base salary, most of her pay came from commissions and she apparently had a knack for selling on the phone. Some of her checks for working part time were bigger than I got for working full time and I did make good money. Our money problems from before were not because I didn't make enough money to support my family, but because I couldn't buy Rae all the things she wanted and desired. She loved buying new clothes, jewelry, and gadgets. We had a pretty good VCR, but when the new ones came out with four track heads we just had to have one. Couldn't wait until the old one went bad and then get the new one - no sir - get the new one right now! Wide screen TV, DVD, HDTV, you name it and if it was the newest thing, we just had to have it and right now. Well, with her new job she was in her glory; so much new stuff was finding its way into our house that I began to think I would have to build an addition to store it all. But Rae was happy, I was getting laid again - life was good.

The next months passed quickly by and I began to notice a change in Rae. It was so gradual that it hadn't registered right away, but one day I noticed that Rae always seemed to be horny. As I mentioned, our sex life got better when she went to work, but by that I meant we went from zip to twice and sometimes three times a week. Somewhere over the course of the last six months it had gone from two or three times a week to three and sometimes four and then from four and sometimes five to six and sometimes seven times a week. She would come home from work and if I were asleep she would wake me up to make love. If I were awake and watching the TV she would walk over and turn it off and nod toward the bedroom. And she was always hot and wet when I slid into her.

Like I said, it was a gradual thing and it really didn't register until one day I stayed home from work to get some jobs done around the house. Those few jobs never even got touched. The kids were in school, Rae and I were home alone, and she couldn't keep her hands off me. We made love five times before she went to work and twice after she got home. She wasn't that passionate on our honeymoon and at that time I'd thought she was a wild woman. I wondered what had happened to her to turn her into a sex maniac, not that I really cared because I was loving it.

Rae had gone from working six hours a day, four days a week to six or seven hours on five days a week with an occasional Saturday thrown in. There were times when she would go in early because they were shorthanded, but she was almost always home by ten. Sometimes she would stop after work to have drinks with her co-workers and didn't get home until midnight, but I didn't think anything of it and life would have gone on being good if one of the guys I worked with hadn't hit the lottery.

Jimmy won 1.3 million after taxes and he invited the whole crew to go out and celebrate with him. It was a spur of the moment thing and Rae had already gone to work so I had to scramble to come up with a sitter for the kids. Jimmy took us to a place called the Palomino Club, which was an upscale strip club that he liked to frequent.

"They got the best looking babes in town dancing here and most of them make pretty good money on the side if you know what I mean," and he gave a big wink.

Jimmy said the night was on him. "Babes, booze, whatever, you don't put your hands in your pockets for nothing."

The booze part was all right with me, but I had no intention of taking him up on the babes part, at least not when we first got there. Jimmy spent lavishly and got several tables put together right down in front of the stage, arranged for a tab, and we settled in to enjoy ourselves. He was right, the place did have some great looking women dancing there and when the girl would finish her set, she would get down off the stage and mingle with the crowd. She would sit with customers or give lap and table dances to whoever was willing to pay for the privilege and every once in a while the girl and a customer would disappear into a back room for a private performance. We had seen three girls since we had arrived and according to Jimmy there were six in the rotation.

"Wait until you see the next one," he said. "She's the hottest babe here. Fucks like a mink and can suck a tennis ball through a garden hose. You can have whichever one you want and I'm paying. Marla is mine."

Just then, as if on cue, the voice over the loudspeaker system said, "And now here she is, The Marvelous Miss Marla!" The music started playing and she was everything that Jimmy said and I sat there rooted to my seat as she pranced around the stage wearing high heels and two pieces of imagination which some people might call a bikini and others might call shadows caused by the stage lights. My cock got rock hard immediately and I sat there open mouthed and stared at her for all of her three songs. When the music was over, she came down off the stage and headed for our table. She sat down on Jimmy's lap and said:

"Been missing me, sugar?"

"You know I have, baby. I'm ready for some private time, are you?"

She smiled at him and said, "Let me have a drink first, lover. It gets awfully hot up there with those stage lights on my body. Give a girl some time to catch her breath, okay?"

She started looking around the table and when her eyes met mine, Rae knew she was busted. We held each other's gaze and I could read the emotions that passed over her face. First surprise, then guilt, followed by resignation, and then determination. She might be going down in flames, but she would damn well do it with her colors flying. She downed her drink, took Jimmy by the hand, and looking me straight in the eye said:

"Come on, sugar. Let's get you your private show," and she led him over to the door that went into the back.

Other girls came out and danced, but I didn't see them because my eyes never left the door that Jimmy and Rae had gone through. It was twenty minutes before they came out and Jimmy headed for the table while Rae went backstage. About five minutes later The Marvelous Miss Marla danced another set and, as the first time, my eyes never left her. When she was done she headed for our table again. This time she walked up to me and said:

"Got room on your lap for me, sailor?"

I moved my chair back to make room for her and she sat down on my hard on. Her eyebrows went up and she stole Mae West's line, "Is that a roll of quarters in your pants, or are you just happy to see me?"

The guys at the table all cracked up and Rae said, "You like watching Miss Marla dance" and I said that I did. "Would you like a private showing?"

I looked at my watch and saw that it was almost nine o'clock. "Normally I would say yes, but I need to be home when my wife gets there so I need to be leaving."

I looked around the table, and to this day I don't know why I did it, but I pointed to Billy Neubert, "He looks like he might be willing to kill for the privilege." Rae gave me a long look and then she got up and took Billy by the hand and led him to the door. Jimmy looked at me and said:

"Are you nuts? Turning something like that down?"

I shrugged my shoulders. "Jimmy, my wife would kill me if she found out that I did something like that, and believe me when I say she would find out."

I thanked him for his generosity and I headed on home.

Once home I paid the sitter, put the kids to bed and then I waited. For what I wasn't sure, but I waited. Would Rae come home at her usual time, or would tonight be one of her late nights? Would she even come home? And if and when she did, what was going to happen? She obviously wasn't tele-marketing like she told me. Why had she lied? There was nothing wrong with being a dancer, if that's all she did. I may have been a little naïve, but there were laws about not being able to touch the dancers. True, Jimmy did say that she fucked like a mink, but Jimmy was one of those 'good ole boys' who liked to brag about what studs they were and it could have been all bullshit.

The only thing that I knew for sure was that The Marvelous Miss Marla wasn't the Rae Ann Keifer that I had married. Rae Ann Chotin nee Keifer wouldn't even wear a bikini at the beach; she wore a one-piece suit that covered everything. My wife Rae Ann didn't even own a pair of high heels, let alone a pair of the 'come fuck me' pumps she danced in.

I'd watched other girls while they had been doing table and lap dances, and while there was lewd and suggestive behavior, I hadn't seen any actual touching. But what went on in those privacy rooms? At ten after ten I heard the garage door opener start up and a couple of minutes later Rae came into the living room. She was still wearing her 'come fuck me' heels and her dancer's costume:

"Miss Marla wants your cock, sailor. You going to help her out?"

She started walking toward the bedroom and every question I wanted to ask was forgotten as I watched her walk toward the bedroom in those high heels. It was the most intense sex I'd ever experienced. I fucked The Marvelous Miss Marla five times that night. Every time I thought I was done and couldn't possibly get it up again, I thought of her sitting on Jimmy's lap and then going through the door to the privacy room with him and with Billy and I was on her again. I finally fell into an exhausted sleep at two in the morning.

When the clock went off to get me up for work in the morning, Rae was snoring so I let her sleep and got ready for work. This was Rae's day off and our talk would wait until I got home from work. It was a bad day at work. Every time I saw Jimmy (he wasn't going to quit his job just because he hit the lottery) or Billy, I saw Rae walking into the privacy room with them and as much as I wanted to, I could not bring myself to ask them what had happened in the room. I was a wreck when I punched out to go home. I walked into the house to find a note on the kitchen table:

"Sailor - One of the girls called in sick and they asked me to come in and cover for her. Should be home by ten." And she signed it MMM. There was a PS: "Those heels seemed to do something for you. I'll wear them again tonight."

The kids got home from school and I fixed them an early dinner and then found a sitter for them. At six-thirty I was sitting at a table in the back of the Palomino Club. The MMM was on stage when I got there and when her set was over she came down to mingle with the customers. I saw her take some money from a guy and then give him a lap dance. She left that table and went over to another and after a couple of minutes she took a guy by the hand and led him to the back room. Ten minutes later they came back out and she went back stage to get ready for her next set. All in all she danced four sets while I sat there and watched. She did five more lap dances and made three more trips to the back room before I had to get up and leave. Rae got home at ten-twenty and walked into the living room wearing only her high heels. That night was a repeat of the previous night except I only fucked her four times before falling asleep.

The morning was also a repeat of the previous morning, but even though Rae had to work that night the next day was Saturday so I wouldn't have to get up and leave. Just before I left the bedroom she gave a loud yawn and I saw her eyes open. I looked at the clock and saw that I was running late and I bent down and kissed her and she rolled over and went back to sleep.

That afternoon Jimmy offered to take us to the Palomino Club again, but only Billy and I took him up on his offer. I made some quick calls to arrange for a sitter and five o'clock found us sitting at a table down front. When we got there TMMM was performing a lap dance at a table with three guys and soon one of them got up and followed her to the back room. When she came out twenty minutes later Jimmy got her attention and she waved at him before going back stage. Five minutes later she did her set and then came to our table and sat down on Jimmy's lap:

"Been missing me, sugar?"

Jimmy told her not to be wasting her time on the other tables that night. "I'm playing big spender tonight, baby, and we want you all to ourselves. Ain't that right, boys?"

Billy said, "That's right, Jimmy," and I just sat there with my eyes on Rae as she smiled back at me. Two minutes later she led Jimmy off to the back room. After the next set, she took Billy and then it was my turn. She came down off the stage, walked over to me and sat down on my lap:

"You have to rush home again tonight, sailor, or would you like a little bit of privacy with Miss Marla?"

Jimmy laughed and said, "You'd better go. It ain't all that often that I'm going to be paying for your fun."

Rae smiled at me. "You want some fun, sailor? It might be a kick for you to visit Miss Marla on somebody else's nickel."

I didn't resist when she pulled me out of the chair. I felt all the eyes in the club on me as Rae led me to the back door. Once through the door I saw that it actually opened onto a long hallway and that there were several doors on either side of the hallway, each with a girl's name on it. The door at the very end had Marla on it and once inside I saw we were in a room that was 7' x 7' and all that was there was a chair and a rather substantially built table. There was a loudspeaker mounted on the wall and the music that the girls danced to was coming out of it. Rae pointed at the chair and I went over and sat down on it.

"Unbutton your fly, sailor, and take out your cock."

I did as she said and she stepped out of her costume, such as it was, and started doing a lap dance. As she wriggled and moved over my lap the hairs of her pussy brushed the head of my cock and her nipples touched my face.

"Like it, sailor? Like the idea that The Marvelous Miss Marla is so close that you can almost put yourself in her?" and she pushed down so that briefly her mound touched the head of my dick. Did I want my dick in her, hell yes I did and I told her so. Rae giggled and said:

"It's against the rules for me to let you do that, sailor, but if you can keep a secret I might just break the rules for you. Would you like that? Would you like Miss Marla to break the rules for you?"

I said yes and she said, "Enough to tip Miss Marla two hundred if she was to suck your cock? Or would you rather tip her three hundred for her hot wet pussy?"

"I want both," I said and she laughed.

"That's good sailor, let's spend Jimmy's money."

She went to her knees and took my dick in her mouth and in less than two minutes I shot my load down her throat and she just kept on sucking until I had a hard dick again.

"Come on, sailor," and she pulled me up and I found out why the table was so sturdily built. She laid down on it and said, "Come on, sailor, help Miss Marla break the rules."

When it was over she put her costume back on and left me there in the room. She made two more trips to the room with Jimmy and one more with Billy and then she came up to us following her last set and sat down on my lap.

"My car isn't running right, sailor. Give a girl a ride home? You can stay and play for a while if you want, Jimmy's paying, right Jimmy?"

And Jimmy didn't know what to say. Finally he stammered, "That's what I said, that the night was on me."

Rae got up and said, "Meet you out back, sailor."

As she walked away Jimmy said, "What you got that's so special? I've been trying to get her to leave with me for six months now and she keeps she's not allowed to date customers."

I shrugged. "Just my natural charm I guess."

My mind was in turmoil as I went around to the back of the building to meet Rae. Until tonight I had convinced myself that Rae was just a dancer and that the privacy rooms were just a place for a more blatant form of lap dance, like what mine started out to be. And now I had to face the fact that Rae was selling herself for money. Or was she? Did I get sucked and fucked because I was her husband, but everybody else got the blatant lap dance? There were only two ways to find out - ask someone who went in there with her or ask Rae herself. But would she tell me the truth? Would she tell me that everybody got to break the rules with Miss Marla, or would she say that everyone else just got the X-rated lap dance and let my imagination run wild?

Rae was waiting for me at the back door. "Nothing wrong with my car, sailor. I just thought it would be a kick to have Jimmy pay me for fucking my own husband. Race you home."

As I drove home I reflected on what Rae had said and to me it sure sounded like she was fucking for money, and that gave me a whole new set of questions that I needed to ask.

Chapter 2

Rae's words bounced around in my head as I drove home:

"I thought it would be a kick to have Jimmy pay me to let my own husband fuck me."

Was that an admission that she was fucking for money or was she jerking my chain? And if she was selling herself, what did that say about me? The thought was certainly on my mind the first night I saw her go into the privacy rooms with Jimmy and Billy and yet when she came home I had fucked her until I was exhausted. The very next night, I had sat in the back of the club and watched as after each dance set she had gone into the privacy rooms with somebody and that night again I couldn't keep my hands off of her.

My next thought was mind boggling - at the cheapest rate (according to what Rae had quoted me, two hundred for a blow job) she had made at least a grand that night. No wonder she always seemed to be able to go out and spend to her heart's content.

She was waiting for me in bed when I got home. She was naked except for her high heels and she was running a finger in and out of her pussy.

"Hurry up, sailor. Miss Marla's pussy is hot, wet, and hungry for a cock."

For the third night in a row I could not keep my hands off her and finally we both fell asleep exhausted. I awoke with a warm mouth on my cock and I looked down to see Rae looking up at me. As soon as she saw that I was awake she stopped sucking and climbed up and sat on me. She looked down at me:

"So, baby, how do you like being married to a whore?"

I looked up at her face and was silent - mostly because I couldn't think what to say.

"Come on, baby, tell me what you're thinking. You know what I'm doing when I go back into that room. I'm a slut, a whore, and I love it. Come on, baby, talk to me, talk to your whore. Do you like fucking me when I come home after fucking strangers?"

I twisted my body and rolled on top of her and started slamming my cock into her.

"That's it, baby, fuck me, fuck your slutty wife. Harder, baby, fuck me harder," and I pounded into her as hard as I could and when I came I collapsed on top of her, rolled off and started up at the ceiling.

"Why? Why are you doing it?"

She came up on an elbow and looked at me:

"Because I love it, baby. I love it and I just can't seem to get enough cock. No matter how much I get, I always seem to want more."

I asked her how long she had been doing it and how she got started and she told me the story.

She had gone out and got the job with a telemarketing firm and for three months she'd sold time-shares in condominiums over the phone. One day she had was called into the boss's office and he had asked her if she would like to make twice as much money for doing the same kind of work. Naturally Rae was interested and when she'd said yes he had handed her a script and asked her to read it out loud. She read it to herself and said:

"I can't read this to you, I'm a married woman."

He had explained to her that she didn't have to mean it, just sound like she did. She was hesitant, but eventually he had talked her into doing it.

"Oh God, you have me so hot that I wish you were here so I could suck your cock."

The boss told her that it wasn't bad and to try it again putting emphasis here, lowering her voice a little there, and after a half dozen tries he said:

"Good! I think that's got it. Let's field test it," and he dialed a number. "Morty? I think I've got something here. Give a listen."

He handed the phone to Rae and told her to read the line just the way they had settled on to the guy on the phone. She did and so started her career as a 900 number girl - "I'll suck you dry. 99cents a minute, call 1-900-760-SUCK. Must be 18 or older."

She was a natural at it and there was a by-product - she got so horny talking to the callers that she came home and took it out on me. A couple of months went by and the boss called her into his office again. He had a couple of friends that he used as quality control. They would call in acting as customers and see how the girls were doing. One of them had called in and had talked with Rae and her voice had, as he had put it to her boss, made his spine tingle and he wanted to meet her. When Rae had looked confused her boss had said:

"What he wants is to have sex with you."

Rae had gotten indignant and her boss had told her to calm down. "I'm not saying that you have to do it and your job doesn't depend on it, but most of you girls are here for the money and George gave the last girl who tingled his spine a thousand bucks for six hours of her time. You do what you want to do; all I'm doing here is passing on information."

Rae agreed to meet the man for coffee; they met, talked, and the next day, which was her day off, she spent from noon until ten that night with him. He was partial to blow jobs and she had sucked him off several times, fucked him several times and had come home with twelve hundred dollars in her purse. She had enjoyed it so much that when George had called her two weeks later she had done it again. For the next two months she had seen George once every two weeks or so and had never left with under a grand in her purse.

"And it wasn't just the money, baby, I was loving the hell out of the sex."

One night when she had gone to meet George there was another guy there and George told Rae that the other guy, Tony, wanted to offer her a job at his club. She talked with Tony and decided to take the job and before she left she had fucked both of them several times and had come home with fourteen hundred dollars. She gave her notice and her boss had tried to talk her into staying with him, but she had made up her mind. He told her he was sorry to lose her and had been so nice about it that she had given him a blow job and then fucked him on his desk.

Her job at the Palomino Club was supposed to be as a hostess, serving drinks and taking care of Tony and George who was Tony's partner. One night two of the dancers hadn't showed up and Tony talked her into dancing and the rest was history. For the last six months she had been taking turns fucking Tony and George with the other girls, dancing and making trips to the privacy rooms with guys who turned her on. Not just anyone who asked, but with the ones who grabbed her interest:

"Believe it or not, baby, but there have been nights, a lot of them, when I haven't gone into the back room."

For example, she said she never would have gone back there with Billy because he just didn't appeal to her. I had pointed at him and in effect had said to her, "Fuck that one" and so she had. The first time with George was for the money, but then she found that she liked fucking other men. The fact that she was cheating on me didn't bother her because she knew I'd never find out about it. I just wasn't the kind of guy who went to places like the Palomino and besides, wasn't she already fucking me to death when she got home?

I had to ask, "Why, if you are having so much fun fucking all these other men and making all that money, are you hanging around here? Why haven't you dumped me for somebody like Jimmy? He's a millionaire and he's crazy about you."

She got a hurt look on her face, "I would have thought you wouldn't have to ask that."

"Why's that?" I wanted to know.

"Because, asshole, I love you and I like being married to you. As far as Jimmy and his money are concerned, I'll be getting it from him a thousand dollars at a time." She saw the look on my face. "What? You expect me to stop just because you found out? After the way you have behaved these last three nights? If you wanted me to stop why didn't you do it that first night just before Jimmy took me into the back room? You're not stupid, baby, you knew, even if you didn't want to admit it to yourself, what was going on in those back rooms. You knew what was going to happen when you pointed at Billy and you knew you were going to be fucking a freshly fucked wife when I got home that night and you loved it! You couldn't leave me alone.

"I saw you the other night, sitting in the back of the club and watching what I did and you couldn't keep your hands off me that night either. Last night you knew for sure what was going on and you still came after me like a sex maniac. Why should I quit now? I'm loving every minute of what I'm doing and so far so do you."

She had me there. For the last three nights I couldn't leave her alone and I was already hard again from just talking about it and Rae noticed. She reached over and started stroking me:

"Tell the truth, baby, hasn't the fact that your wife is a cock loving slut made you want me more?" I was silent, trying to get my thoughts together and she said, "Come on, baby, talk to me."

Finally I said, "Well, working with Billy and Jimmy every day while knowing that they are fucking you is not easy. Every time I see them I picture you walking into the back room with them and I end up walking around with a hard dick all day."

Rae giggled, she actually giggled, and said, "That's just the way I want you, baby. I want you with a hard dick waiting for me to come home to you."

***

The Marvelous Miss Marla still works at the Palomino Club four and sometimes five nights a week and I'm still waiting for her with a hard dick when she comes home. Jimmy still takes the crew to the club once a month or so and when he does The Marvelous Miss Marla always asks me to take her home and as a result I'm looked upon as some kind of stud to the rest of the guys. It does bother me a little to help Rae spend the money she makes from her job, but I'm starting to get used to it, but we do have a problem coming up in the near future. The company Christmas party is fast approaching and Rae is expecting me to take her, but she won't tell me if she is planning to go as The Marvelous Miss Marla or as Mrs. Rae Chotin. Should be an interesting night either way.

~~The End~~

Here is a sample from another story you may enjoy:

Just Plain Bob

Sharing Penny

hot wife sharing erotica

It was my fault and I admit it. I accept the blame. I take responsibility for my actions. I own up to being the cause, the driving force behind it all. It was my idea, I pursued it, I encouraged it, and the blame is mine. None of that makes it any easier to wake up in the morning and find myself alone in bed.

***

It started with an overheard conversation in the lunchroom at work. Frank and Ernie were sitting at the table next to mine and they were talking about two of our co-workers, Bill and Steve. Ernie is a little hard of hearing so Frank was trying to speak loud enough for Ernie to hear him while at the same time trying not to talk so loud that everyone else could hear what he was saying. As a result I was hearing what they were talking about.

"She actually fucked him with Steve sitting there watching?"

"That's what Bill said."

"Do you believe him?"

"Why not? He isn't the first one it has happened to. George in Purchasing and Mike and Sam in Accounting have done her. Apparently Steve gets his jollies watching other men fuck her and then he goes down on her when they are done."

"He eats her cunt with another man's cum in her?"

"That's the story I get."

"Ooh, gross!"

"I don't know about that. Have you seen his wife? I've heard guys say they would eat a mile of her shit just to be able to kiss where it came from."

"No, I've never seen her, but it wouldn't matter how good looking she was I couldn't suck on her cunt with another guy's junk in her."

Well I knew Steve's wife and I could honestly say that as much as I love my wife I would have to seriously consider Marsha's cum filled pussy if it would lead to my being able to fuck her. For the rest of the day as I did my job I wondered how Steve went about selecting lovers for Marsha. Or did Marsha choose and send Steve out to fetch? Whatever the selection process, it was obvious that I wasn't anywhere on the list. I had known them both for several years and they had socialized with me and my wife Penny. We have had dinner at their place and they have attended barbecues at our house and I'd never known or even had a hint that they had a kinky side. But this isn't about Steve, Marsha and me; it is about Penny and me.

***

I was still thinking about Steve watching Marsha fuck other men when I started home that night and about halfway home a stray thought entered my head. I wondered how a man could watch his wife, just sit there and pay rapt attention, as another man drove his cock into her and made her squeal and moan and I knew one thing for sure – I couldn't do it! At least that is what I told myself, but for the next couple of weeks it seemed to be all I could think of.

In my mind I pictured Marsha on a bed getting plowed by me while Steve sat next to the bed and smiled as Marsha screamed out in pleasure. I saw me standing off to the side watching Steve suck my cum out of his wife while my dick grew hard and then I fucked her again. I was not even aware of it when the change occurred, but one day I woke up to the fact that the picture in my mind was of Penny on the bed and me on the chair and that I had an aching hard on. From that point on I spent a lot of time wondering if I could actually watch someone else fuck my wife and if it would be a turn on. Not that I would ever know because there just wasn't anyway on God's Green Earth that Penny or I would ever do anything like that.

If you enjoyed this sample, look for **<u>Sharing Penny</u>**.

Also by this Author:

The Prodigal Family: The Abbotts

Watching My Shared Wife

The Waitress and the Runaway Husband

Baiting Mr. Little

Too Hot for Henry

Chuck's Fantasy

The Redhead's Desires

Rescued at Riley's

His Every Fantasy

Open Mike Night

Pursuit for Revenge

Why Does He Do That?

Halloween & Drugs

Tracey

When Rob Met Kari

Becoming a Shared Wife, Vol. 1 –
(Wife Sharing and Other Adventures)

Becoming a Shared Wife, Vol. 2 –
(Hazardous Wives)

Becoming a Shared Wife, Vol. 3 –
(Wives Who Stray)

Erotica Short Stories, Vol. 8 –

(Wild Urges)

Erotica Short Stories, Vol. 9 –

(Horny)

A Weird One

Blackmailed MILF

Filthy Steps With My...

Stuffed Hard

The Biggest She's Ever Had

9 Shades of Sex

Sharing Penny

From the Author

WANT FREE COPIES OF MY BOOKS?
Just visit my blog and download free copies of my books:
awesomeauthors.org/justplainbob

If you enjoyed any of my books then please share the love and promote my books in Amazon.

If you write me a review and send me an email I will send you a free book, or many.
(Just know that these emails are filtered by my publisher.)

Good news is always welcome.

One Last Thing, For Kindle Readers...

When you turn the page, Kindle will give you the opportunity to rate this book and share your thoughts on Facebook and Twitter. If you enjoyed my writings, would you please take a few seconds to let your friends know about it? Because... when they enjoy they will be grateful to you and so will I.

Thank You!

An Open Letter from Just Plain Bob

A message for those who like my stories, those who hate my stories, those who are indifferent and those who have yet to make up their minds.

I have often stated that I really don't care what others think about my stories, that I write for my own enjoyment and then I offer to share. If you like my stories fine and if you don't, also fine since I have already satisfied my target audience - me!

It is human nature to strive to get better. If you take up bowling your first games are going low scoring, but you will work and practice to get better and as your average climbs you may forget the game where you had three gutter balls and shot an eighty-six, but that game is still there in your past.

Your first time on the golf course you shot an eighty on the front nine, but did you settle for that being your game or did you work to improve? You may eventually get a three handicap, but that nine hole eighty is still there as part of your past.

When you hired in at your job did you say, "Cool, I got it made" and do nothing more than what you barely had to do or did you go to work thinking that, "Someday I'm going to be running this place." You might never climb that high, but human nature says that you are going to at least try.

It is the same with authors who write stories and post them on sites like Literotica. Their first stories might not be all that good, but comments and feedback along with a desire to get better drive them toward putting out a better product or to at least try.

I'm no different. My first stories might not have been all that great, but they are still there on the hard drive. I like cheating wife stories and five years ago I found my first adult site that catered to cheating wife stories. It was a pay site, but it had a policy of giving a free lifetime membership to anyone who submitted five stories to the site. How hard can that be I said to myself as I sat down and fired up the word processor and went to work.

I sent my five stories in and sat back to enjoy my free membership and a funny thing happened. I started getting feedback, most of it positive, and I became hooked. I started cranking out more stories. The site I was sending my stories to had seven categories:

Bisexual
Cream Pie

Groups
I Watch
Gang Bang
Racial
SM/BD

I know nothing about bisexual or SM/BD and I had no interest in Groups so all the stories I wrote I tailored for the four remaining categories:

Cream Pie
I Watch
Gang Bang
Racial.

I turned out eight stories a month, two for each category, which means that after five years I have over 120 stories in each of those categories and they are all still on the hard drive.

A year ago I received an email asking me why I never posted stories on Literotica. The answer? I didn't know about Lit. I pulled it up, liked what I saw, and started sending in stories to it. All new stories? No, not hardly, not with over 400 stories sitting on the hard drive. Maybe one new story for each fifteen or so old ones. The newer ones are better, at least I think they are and I have received some feedback that leads me to believe that others think so too, and I will continue to write new ones.

But I am still going to recycle what is on the hard drive, stories that were written specifically to fit the four categories. That means that those of you who hate cream pie stories still have eighty or so to look forward to. Ditto for those who call me a racist; you will get another seventy or so interracial stories.

Those who hate wimps will only see about fifty more of those because the stories I sent to the I Watch category were split 50/50 between what some call wimps and some call "real men." Why the 50/50 split? It came from listening to the readers. I would get feedback asking me why all the men in my stories were hard asses. "In real life men are more forgiving, especially if it is the first indiscretion." So I would write stories with forgiving husbands and boyfriends and then the next batch of feedback would say, "Why are all your husbands spineless wimps" and I'd write stories that went back the other way.

Eventually I came to realize that I was wasting my time - there was no way I could write a story that would satisfy everybody and that is when I adopted my philosophy of writing for my own enjoyment and then offering to share.

As far as the gangbang stories? Well, what can I say? Gangbangs are gangbangs and there are still eighty or so of them to go.

The bottom line is that Literotica readers are going to see more of my old stories than my new ones. If I'm still around three or four years from now it will probably go the other way, more new than old.

I feel the need to respond to some of the comments and emails I have received. By far the largest percentage comes from people who say, "You are an asshole because all women are not whores and sluts and that's all you make them out to be."

Next most common is, "You must really hate women you sick fuck."

"You must be a wimp because all the men in your stories are wimps" is up there in the top ten along with, "Why don't you give it a rest and go crawl off in a hole somewhere."

There is a lot more, but I'm only going to address those four and in reverse order.

I won't stop and go crawl in a hole because I am enjoying the hell out of what I am doing and remember what I said, I am doing this for MY OWN ENJOYMENT and then I offer to share. Some obviously like my sharing with them and so I will continue to do so. No one is holding a gun to a reader's head and telling them they must click on a Just Plain Bob story or die. It is a conscious choice on the reader's part to move that mouse and click on that story.

When a man finds out he has a cheating wife or girlfriend there are only a limited number of ways he can handle it. If he loves her he can forgive, try to forget and try to hold on and somehow make things work. He can turn his back on her, walk away and get on with his life. The third option is to take revenge.

According to a good portion of those who send me feedback the first and second options are proof that the men are wimps. If the man takes the third option he is still considered a wimp if he doesn't do some sort of physical damage to the woman and her lover. These readers believe that the only way not to be a wimp is to kill, maim and destroy everything in sight. Doing that however, will invariably get the man throw in jail and that is why it so rarely happens in real life.

In real life most revenge takes place in the man's head when he says to himself, "I should have _____ (fill in the blank) the fucking cunt!" I know this because I have been there and done that (see The Dark Trilogy). In my stories I try to mirror real life so kill, maim and destroy are going to be for the most part absent. Outside of some fisticuffs there will be very little physical violence in my stories. Most of my husbands are going to do what I did, what several of my friends and others that I know have done, forgive, or walk away. If this makes them wimps and me a wimp for writing the story that way, so be it.

Next is the "I must hate all women." Nothing could be farther from the truth. I love women. I lust after women. I even like whores and sluts. I have been married four times, engaged two other times (that did not end in marriage) and I have always had girlfriends between marriages. My philosophy is that women were put on this earth for me to enjoy and I'm not talking just sexually. I could sit at the mall (and have) for hours and just girl watch.

The engagements, girlfriends and three of the four marriages bring me to the #1 anti JPB comment on the list.

"You are an asshole because all women aren't whores and sluts."

Well dear reader, you can not prove that by me! I will say up front that I KNOW all women aren't whores and sluts, BUT the majority of the women in my life were. My mother ran around on my father for years while he was driving a truck for a living. My Aunt Margaret cheated regularly on my Uncle Bill, as did my Aunt Mildred on my Uncle Paul. My Aunt Betty fucked around on my Uncle Bob for years and finally left him for his brother, my Uncle Wendell. Uncle Wendell in turn caught her on her knees at his company Christmas party giving Season's Greetings to his boss.

My sister is three times divorced and each divorce came about when the then current husband caught her out spreading pollen. Both of the engagements I mentioned ended when I found out that I was not the one and only and a lot of the girls I dated between marriages never made it to engagement status for the same reason.

And that brings me to my three ex-wives. The first one, Helen (I believe I commented on her in the intro to The Dark Trilogy) had seven different lovers before I found out what was going on. I was living proof that love is blind. Ditto with my second wife. She had a secret life that she hid from me and when I found out about her brother, his friends and the gangbangs she was history.

My third marriage ended in divorce because of a different kind of cheating (and I can just imagine the outrage I am going to get over this) - she cheated on me with an idea. I was away from home on business, she was lonely, a couple of Jehovah's Witnesses knocked on the door and my wife, with nothing better to do invited them in. When I came home from my trip I found out that she had found God. On a scale that runs from TRUE BELIEVER on one end to ATHEIST on the other you will find me just to the right of AGNOSTIC and since I would not allow myself to be SAVED the marriage eventually died.

So yes, I write about sluts and whores because as everyone knows, you tend to write about the things you know. And I do like sluts and whores, just not the ones that lie to me and cheat on me.

So be forewarned - if you click on a Just Plain Bob story you will be getting sluts, whores and husbands who do not kill, maim and destroy. There are other things you will rarely find in a Just Plain Bob story. Even though I try to mirror real life my stories all take place in StoryLand. In StoryLand STDs and un-wanted pregnancies do not exist unless the author feels like they may add something to the story. Bad things do not happen in StoryLand unless the author so wills it and no amount of "You should have…" in comments and feedback will change a story already posted.

Lastly, I will touch on a truth. None of what I have written here means shit because the same readers will still read the same stories that they profess to hate and make the same comments they have always made. Knowing this, I will deliberately post stories that will have them frothing at the mouth.

It is the least I can do for an adoring public.

Thank you!

Just Plain Bob
justplainbob@awesomeauthors.org

You may also like the books by these authors:

JACK RYDER

THE CHEATING GAME

NAUGHTY EROTICA

I can't really remember exactly how I came up with the idea. The WHY is as clear as day, even after all these years. The entire motivation behind my sly little plan was driven by a deep rage fueled lust to get even with a malicious infidelity and to fulfill a childhood fantasy. I had fantasized about my sexy MILF mother-in-law ever since I started dating her daughter way back in high school. I had been leery of my best friend Peter's lust for my wife almost nearly as long. It would ultimately be those two things thrown together by circumstance, that would drive me to make the plan and take the actions that I have.

But I am getting way ahead of myself here. I should start at the beginning, so you may understand why this happened and maybe you won't hate me in the end. It's not like I ruined anyone's life or physically hurt anyone. Although I manipulated some situations, I did not force anyone to do the things they did all by themselves willingly. Although I started some wheels in motion, the results found a momentum of their own. The bottom line is that cheaters cheat and I took full advantage of that.

I would have to say that the event that started the ball rolling, happened the night of my bachelor party. It wasn't a surprise to anyone that Nikki and I were gonna tie the knot. We have been inseparable since we first met on the first day of high school. My best friend Pete has been the only other significant person that has been part of the last three years of our lives, along with Nikki's mom Krysta.

Nikki and I wanted to get married right after graduation, so we would have some time together before she travelled across the state to attend college. We knew the distance would keep us apart for certain amounts of time, but we were both determined to continue our plans so we could build a successful life together. I would stay home and continue working, so I could take over my father's company someday. Nikki would complete her education and someday become my accountant. We had a plan and we were certain that we could make it work.

Pete insisted on throwing a big bachelor party. It was sort of embarrassing that most of the fellows that attended that night were really Pete's friends. Although I knew most of the fellows, they were just mostly acquaintances from various school functions. I had asked Pete to keep the party a low key event, but he went all out anyway. It was my initial feeling that Pete just wanted to seem like a big shot to all his other buddies. It wouldn't be till some time later, that he had an entirely different motive.

It was really your average rented bar sort of bachelor party. Complete with strippers, lap dancers, and a lot of liquor consumption. I was pleased that he had at least thought ahead enough to contact a shuttle bus taxi service to get everyone home safely. I made it a point to not get nearly as drunk as the rest of the fellows. But it seemed like Pete was trying his best to force more drinks on my way even if I left them untouched.

Throughout the evening, each of the strippers made their way over to kiss and rub their mostly nude bodies all over the groom to be. It was very unsettling to me as the fellows took cell phone photos each time they did it. But I didn't make a big deal about it, since they were taking photos of all the girls rubbing all over the other fellows as well. I did notice that Pete seemed to get quite excited each time he took photos of the girls humping on me. He seemed to have a huge grin as he snapped his shots. Just before midnight, shortly after I told Pete I was about ready to go home, one of the strippers pushed me down onto my chair and proceeded to sit on my lap for a lap dance.

The fellows were all whooping and hollering, as she ripped off her top and shoved her big hooters in my face. When I saw the flashes from Pete's camera, I knew how this could look if Nikki ever saw them. As I grasped her hips to lift her off, her unfastened bikini bottom fell off and Pete snapped a photo with her nude body pressed against mine.

If you enjoyed this sample then look for **The Cheating Game**.

GREEN-EYED
Lucy
RESIST ME

GEORGE X. BUSH

My name is Dan and this is the story of how I became my wife's slave. I know that sounds strange, and believe me, when you learn the whole story, you'll *know* it's strange. Even to this day, when I think about everything that's happened in the last 10 years, I don't believe it. But then again, reality has a way of rearing its ugly head and reminding you of what's real and what's not.

I guess a little background is in order. I was born into a very wealthy east-coast family. And they were very conservative. My grandfather had been a senator and my father a two-term governor. My mother was a Mayflower descendant and a power in the highest of the social orders in which our lives revolved. I went to the best prep schools, then Yale and finally the Wharton School of Economics.

When I was young, I was always the biggest guy in my class. Today, I stand 6'5" and 240 pounds. I played all sports and usually ended up being the team captain. I won so many letters in sports that they wouldn't fit on my sweaters. I had many offers of scholarships to college, both academic and athletic. I was an All-American athlete in college football and basketball.

I had literally won the lucky sperm club lottery. I was incredibly blessed in all ways. I never got less than an A in all of my schooling. That's straight A's right through my Master's degree in economics. I'm not bragging, just trying to let you realize that I am not some weirdo from a disadvantaged background, some sort of a physical or psychological weakling that was easily led astray.

I also managed to be myself, making it a point to avoid discussing family and things of that nature, always keeping my responses vague. I had learned early on that people were usually far too impressed by who my family was and that led them to overlook who I actually was. So the few people who actually knew who I was gave me the space to be myself and kept the secret so that I could have as normal a college life as possible.

As I was growing up, girls just seemed to be a part of everything. Being the big sports hero made it possible for a parade of girls to be always available. But I had one problem that was sort of two-edged. My cock is just over 10 inches, and most girls, while very eager to see it and play with it, were just unable to handle all of it. I never saw more than two or three inches of it disappear into a mouth, and never had a girl who would let me bury the whole thing in her pussy. Usually they'd try, some of them several times, but eventually it was just too big and they'd move on.

But word spread and there was never any lack of girls willing to try. Most guys thought I was the luckiest person in the world, but they just didn't know how incredibly frustrating it actually was.

Then I met Lucy just as I was finishing up my Master's degree. Of all places to meet, I met her in a bar I had never been in, just happened to stop in for a beer one day when I was thirsty and had noticed their sign.

Lucy was a waitress. She had very short black hair, sparkling green eyes, a very full set of tits filling her bra, and all in a package just a bit over 5 feet tall. Her personality was so engaging and friendly, a smile seemed to be permanently plastered on her face. She seemed to know everyone by name and obviously liked her job. She was so friendly and seemingly flirty that I actually stammeringly asked her if she'd like to go out sometime. I remember her stopping and really giving me a look-over, slowly, from top to bottom. She had a hand on her chin and was chewing her lower lip as she appraised me before finally nodding and agreeing to go out.

Our first date was one of the best times I ever had with a woman up until then. She turned out to be very well-read and interested in just about everything under the sun. When the day finally ended and I took her home, she shocked me by asking if I'd be interested in spending the night.

She laughed at the astonished look on my face as I stood there with my mouth hanging open. Our date had been purely platonic. There had been no sexual tension at all. Her company had been so stimulating and enjoyable, the usual stuff had just never cropped up.

"It's just that I'm really horny and I thought you might enjoy getting laid," she had said.

"Well, yeah," I stammered. "I just wasn't thinking... I just wasn't expecting..."

If you enjoyed this sample then look for **Green-Eyed Lucy**.

G. Stuart Crane

THE FLOG ZONE

PARANORMAL PRECOGNITION

BDSM Erotic Romance

John Peters didn't know what his first birth was like, but his second one was agonizing. He remembered the pain, the drowsy driver crossing lanes, the sounds of crushing and crumpling metal and glass, the fire, and the screaming of his lungs out as they were seared by the very air he breathed. This passed and he felt a new sensation of someone using his/her hands to move his legs. Then came the hot kiss of a lash, and he felt as if he were being flogged forever when he tried to open his eyes to scream. Then the pain turned to pleasure and as it continued till the lash fell.

The scream came out as a gurgle, a whisper. His eyes opened to see light blue walls all around him and that he was in a bed. A woman in surgical scrubs was moving his legs and feet, stretching them, moving them back and forth at the ankles and knees. The woman was pleasant, not pretty in the formless clothes she wore, but with her red hair back in a short ponytail. Expressive green eyes is now wide and watching him. She had stopped what she was doing and was watching a machine beside him. The steady *beep beep* was replaced by something wilder and erratic.

As soon as the woman lets go of his foot, the sensation of being flogged stopped. The combined sensation of pain and pleasure stopped and the machine keeps beeping at a faster pace. She had rushed to his side, and was watching him struggle to form words with his mouth that no longer seemed to work. The noises coming from his mouth were just gargles and hisses.

She left in a hurry and somehow the presence of the fast beeping machine beside him was not an acceptable trade. Still trying to form words, he croaked for help. Where the heck was he and what was happening?

He managed to move his head a little, and look towards left and right. He was in a hospital ward of some kind and bodies on beds were to the left and right of him. Still with IV bags on stands and tubes everywhere, he was sure that he was unmoved. He tried to move his arms and found his arms free and couldn't move a little, since he was so weak.

Minutes passed, the silence was incredible except for the steady drone of the machines and the low beeping noises from all around him. The silence was replaced by the sound of footfalls. He heard hard soled shoes and squeaky rubber ones on tiled floors, walking in a hurry. A nurse in a white uniform and a man in a lab coat flapping behind were at his side. He was older, judging by the wrinkles and gray hair.

"You are awake?" the man in a lab coat asked.

He tried to say "Yes I am and where am I?" but all that came out was a series of croaks and guttural sounds. He did see a name embroidered on the lab coat stating that his name was D. Burns M.D.

He looked at John a few moments, then told the nurse to get some water and straw. He waited till she returned. He poured some room temperature water in a glass, added the straw, and held it to John's lips.

John sucked in the fluid and his mouth seemed to absorb it before the liquid got to his cheeks. The second pull on the straw was better and it got into his throat with the same effect. The third pull went down his throat and soon the dryness and tickling was gone. He pushed the straw away with his tongue and tried to speak again. This time, it came out in a whisper, but intelligible for his ears, it sounded weak and pitiful. "Where am I and how long have I been here?"

The Doctor had to lean closer to hear him. "We will get to that soon, but do you remember your name?"

John whispered his full name to the doctor, then sighed, this was going to be a memory test. Then, while he could, he rattled off his address and anything else that came to mind including his high school and college. The doctor pulled back to look at him. "And what's the last thing you remember?"

"Car, a big white SUV crossing the center line, I couldn't avoid it. I tried running my car onto the sidewalk, it happened fast, the fire, and me screaming." John managed to whisper. "What about my car?"

If you enjoyed this sample then look for The Flog Zone.

THREESOMES EROTICA
DOUG AND DIANE SERIES, BOOK 1

AND MASSEUSE
Makes Three

IAN MACSWAIN

I am a professional masseuse, and have been for many years. When I say professional, I mean that I do massage strictly with no funny business, or hanky panky. My husband is a successful businessman, so I don't have to work as hard as some of my other LMT friends, but I take my work very seriously. My kids are old enough so that my not being at home when they get home from school is not an issue anymore either. This allows me the freedom to set a pretty flexible schedule.

I have a pair of clients, a husband and wife couple, that I have been massaging for quite a number of years. Doug and Diane are a very active couple with two kids in junior high school. Doug designs websites and Diane owns a floral shop. They do very nicely. Their house is up in the hills on about 10 acres of land, with a spectacular view. We have gotten very friendly over the years, like old friends. When I go to massage them, we usually sit and talk for awhile and have a glass of wine on the deck. They are such regular clients that I leave one of my massage tables at their house; they dedicated a room to it. Our relationship has always been totally professional.

Until recently.

A couple of weeks ago, I got a call from Doug, on the morning of one of our appointments, asking if he could meet me for lunch. This was a bit of an irregular request but we had become close enough client/friends that I agreed and we met at a nice restaurant near his office. We chatted for awhile, about family stuff, some business chit chat until he got around to the point and mentioned their upcoming 17th anniversary; coming up the following weekend. They had both agreed that they wanted to do something really special. Doug seemed very nervous. I asked him what was wrong.

"This is really tough to say," he stammered. "And I don't want to make you feel weird." He paused a while before continuing. "Diane and I both really enjoy your company. We think of you as a good friend, as well as our health professional." I told him that I considered them more than simply clients. "Well, we wanted to,...well, ask you if..." He trailed off again.

"I'm not following." I told him.

"We really don't want to risk our friendship with you." He said slowly. "We wanted to know if...you would consider...getting closer."

"Closer?" I asked, unsure what he meant.

"Well, at the risk of offending you, …" He was starting to hem and haw about our earlier discussion about professionalism with my work, keeping it totally professional. "We were wondering if you would consider indulging us in a more,... sensual,... kind of massage."

"More sensual?" I asked. "You mean sexual?"

"No, no." He stumbled. "Well, unless..." There was a long look between us, wherein I said nothing.

"This is not going, … you know, forget it. I'm sorry if, …" We shared a long fairly awkward silence. I think I know what he was saying, and with any other person, I would be up and out of there already. I knew these people, though. This was not something that would drive me out of my chair as I thought it might. I really liked them and Doug was really embarrassed now.

"Hey. It's okay." I told him, trying to prevent him having the heart attack he appeared to be having. I admit that I was intrigued as to what they might be considering, as a couple. It was their anniversary after all. "Just tell me what's on your mind."

"Diane was in a panic over being the one to ask, but now I wish she was here, …" I simply waited, trying not to look as flustered as I felt. I had only had to deal with these kinds of come-ons a couple of times, and had simply packed my shit and walked out; perhaps a bit stern a response but I wasn't having this discussion with strangers, men.

"Diane and I both really like you. We both think that you're awesome at what you do. And … honestly … we both find you very attractive, and we have both been considering ... you know ... a ... something different." Doug's hands were fluttering as if trying to not say something too outlandish. "Not that you ...", he stammered. I smiled at him.

"When I started in this line of work, I swore that I would never get involved in anything sexual with my clients." He looked a bit sad and ashamed for asking. "Don't get me wrong, I'm very flattered that you are asking. I think that you are both very attractive. Very! I suppose if I was ever to consider something like that, it would probably be with people like you two."

"But, ..." he trailed off. "I hope that you're not offended."

"No. Truly."

"I'm sorry. I really am. I hate to make you feel uncomfortable." I assured him that it was fine; that I wasn't, though secretly I was. My mind was suddenly filled with thoughts of what they might be thinking. I caught myself flashing on both their bodies. I had been their massage therapist for a while and had seen most of them already. Diane's bottom flashed into my mind, unbidden. I had to shake my head to clear it. "Will you still make our appointment tonight?"

I patted his hand. "Of course. Believe me. It's okay." He remained uncomfortable through the rest of lunch and seemed ready as hell to get out of there. The conversation was perfunctory at best; the kids' schooling, the weather; it was agony. I tried to think of something to ease his mind. I didn't want them to be embarrassed for their appointments tonight. He shook my hand rather mechanically when we stepped out onto the street, and he walked away rather briskly. I felt so bad for him. Why I didn't feel worse for myself, I don't know.

I didn't mention my lunch to my husband when I got home, as there wasn't enough time to really get into it. The kids needed feeding and then homework had to be done. I left them in front of the TV as I headed out. Later that evening when I got to their house, I felt like Diane in particular was really embarrassed. It remained that way until we were alone and I was massaging her.

I worked on her in silence until I asked, "Are you okay?"

"Yeah, I'm fine. Why?"

"You seem so quiet."

"Oh, I'm sorry. It's just that … well, I'm a little embarrassed." I asked her about what.

"Well, having Doug ask you to help us with our little … fantasy."

"Oh, please. Don't be embarrassed. Besides, we didn't really get into that much detail."

"I'm sorry for putting you on the spot like that."

"Please don't be." I told her quietly. "Besides, I'm flattered." There was a very long silence for a while, then I asked her, "I was just caught a bit… off guard." She apologized again. I just… keep my business, well… like a business." She said that she totally understood and that she hoped I wouldn't think them weird or anything. "Oh, not at all. What people do behind closed doors..." I was sounding like I was discussing it like I knew their private life. I dropped it.

There was a very long period of silence, while I continued her shoulders and back. "I just don't want you to have the wrong idea about us." She said finally.

"I don't have any idea... It's between you guys."

"It's just a stupid fantasy kind of thing." I didn't ask what. "Perhaps they are better as fantasies anyway." She said at last. I hummed that maybe so. I finished her legs and then held the sheet for her as she rolled over.

"What is your fantasy?" I suddenly blurted, not meaning to. We remained silent for awhile. She then quietly and haltingly told me how they had discussed getting a sensual massage. She was nervous about the details, so I continued to press her gently. She described a scene with soft sexy music, dim lights and lots of candles, and a sexy scene wherein a female masseuse would be topless or nude, and there would be a lot of intimate touching, between all of them. I admitted to myself that it sounded kind of cool and that my husband Josh would probably love such a thing.

She continued that Doug would help massage Diane and then vice versa. She even admitted to being curious about being with another woman. She must have talked for half an hour about what she would like to try and watch her husband try.

I told her that that sounded like a magical anniversary. She admitted that maybe they should keep it as just a fantasy. I asked her if they did want to fulfill this fantasy what they would do about making it happen. She thought they might call an escort service. We left it at that.

Throughout the rest of her massage and Doug's, I kept thinking about them and the way they looked nude. Doug was silent the entire time.

I was becoming intrigued with the idea of them wanting to try something new and erotic; do it together and share the experience. Even after I left their house, I couldn't get it out of my head.

When I got home, the kids were asleep and Josh was reading in bed. I mentioned it to my husband, who was already half-asleep. He told me that it sounded like fun to him, and that I might enjoy it. He rolled

Erotic Romance

Almost

BROKEN

Healed Completely!

Kerry James

Where does life take us? Why is it that when you have settled on one course, fate comes knocking at your door and takes you off on a tangent? That's what happened to me, it seems to keep happening to me. I get used to my life, and then fate throws a surprise my way. Sometimes it is a little tap-tap on the door, at others it's a loud knock. Sometimes it blows the door open, and when it is really serious fate just takes the thing off with its hinges.

I am Jack Hunter. My life to date had been particularly uneventful, although that would depend on your point of view. I had a wife, and a daughter. I also had an affair which while it didn't become the reason for my divorce, soured me sufficiently to seek to split with my wife. I will hold my hand up and acknowledge that I cheated on my wife. Not a good thing to do, but I will say in my defence that because my wife was in love with the bottle; Vodka and Tonic was her favourite so no one could be actually sure whether she was tippling or not; our love life was virtually zero. It's no easy task to make love to someone who reeks of alcohol. Brenda, my wife didn't appear to be bothered by our lack of intimacy, her next drink was far more important. I tried to get her to admit the problem, her Doctor tried, her mother tried, even our daughter, Libby, only three years old but she understood that something was wrong with mummy. Nothing worked. Despair and frustration were taking my self-esteem to new depths so when I had met a rather lovely lady called Deborah it quickly went from acquaintance to friendship to lovers.

Our affair went on for three years. But when I called quits on my marriage, and as you would expect got taken to the cleaners in the resulting divorce, Deborah made it plain that we were not going to be an item. She came round for the sex but nothing else. Sounds like any man's dream, doesn't it? I had sex on tap and no emotional baggage to go with it. But I was one of those men who wanted emotion in a relationship, so eventually I told her it was over.

The legal process in the UK was slow but exacting. It had however problems in making its judgments effective. I had visiting rights with my daughter, which were denied or delayed for spurious reasons. My solicitor would petition the court again and again to enforce the judgment. The court would confirm the judgment but never took action to ensure it was complied with. So slowly I lost touch with my daughter.

I met Jasmine in a supermarket; I actually helped her with the heavy bags. We had coffee, then dinner and eventually we started sleeping together on occasional nights. We went on like this for five years, until one day I got a fixed penalty speeding fine in the post. The location was not one I had driven through for months, so I queried the penalty. The bloody camera was right, it was my car, but at the time I had been away at a trade show, and I had travelled to the show by train. There was only one person who had access to my house, and the keys to the company car. Jasmine! After a lot of heated arguments she admitted she had 'borrowed' the car. Problem was that she was not insured to drive it, a criminal offence in the UK. If she admitted the offence to the police, chances were that she would certainly be banned from driving, and get a hefty fine. There was also an outside chance of a prison sentence. I paid the fine, took the points on my licence, and Jasmine became history.

A few months after that lesson, I was invited to a party at a friend's house, which was where I met Bridget. We were under no illusions that we had been invited by well-meaning friends who thought that being single was an offence against nature. Well we did hit it off. Remaining friends for nearly ten years, but the tingle was just not there.

If you enjoyed this sample then look for **Almost Broken**.

WANT FREE COPIES OF MY BOOKS?

Just visit my blog and download free copies of my books:

awesomeauthors.org/justplainbob

over and turned out the light, but that comment kept me up half the night. It sounded like fun to him. And what did he mean I might enjoy it?

If you enjoyed this sample then look for **And Masseuse Makes Three**.